# Night Panther

# Also by Darrel Sparkman

# Night Panther

## Spirit Trail
### Book 2

## Darrel Sparkman

WOLFPACK
PUBLISHING
— EST 2013 —

*To those Native Americans in my extended family holding a rich heritage of old blood.*
*To my immediate family for their untiring support, whose blood is equally old.*
*May those be entwined forever to forge the future.*

# Night Panther

...but never shall you see these realms again,
Darkened by boundless groves,
And roamed by savage men.

*A Walk at Sunset* — *1887*
William Cullen Bryant

# Chapter One

REGARDLESS OF WHERE YOU ARE OR WHAT YOU ARE doing, daydreaming can get you killed. When you're in dense cover and canopied forest along the border between Missouri and Arkansas, it's almost guaranteed. Death can happen in an instant with no warning, but the pain of your last dying breath. The agent of your demise could be bear or panther, a misstep resulting in broken bones, or an ambush by men protecting a perceived hunting domain. Many travelers offering a friendly hand in greeting died on the spot.

In the year 1821, the law was what you made it and could enforce—except for an occasional undermanned Army outpost filled with green troops who looked at the forests and denizens therein as mystical and foreboding, stuff of fairy tales told on the knee of their elders. Few of the soldiers, often conscripts brought over from Ireland or England, had any knowledge of the environment around them.

In Sean MacLeod's mind, on a hot and muggy day, he was already building his new trading post and mill on the slow-moving river he'd found, thinking of using a water wheel to run a saw and grist mill. Milled lumber would be in high demand by settlers—given he could get a belt brought in from Saint Louis. Some made them from rawhide made pliable with oil and grease, but those didn't last long. He'd seen a mill that used only wheels with wooden cogs that meshed together. It was much more efficient, but he didn't know how to build them. Under heavy use, the wooden wheels often split and might take months to replace. Perhaps placing the wheel horizontal to the ground and using a mule or donkey to turn it would be feasible.

Putting a damper on his thoughts, the slate-gray sky dropped rain in a mind-numbing hiss that silenced all other sounds. In a few moments, the only thing keeping him awake on his gently moving horse was the occasional steam of water down the back of his buckskin shirt, runoff from his sodden hat. Once soaked, buckskin clothing became slick and then hardened into a scratchy garment hard as iron.

He followed a meandering game trail in a generally southern direction. There were no roads in this part of the country, no path directly to anywhere. Trails meandered around steep hills and along twisty creeks. You could make your own trail, but unless you needed exercise there was no reason. Forest animals had been doing it since the beginning of time and had already done most of the work, scouting the easiest and most proficient way. The scent of honeysuckle and cedar released by the warm rain lulled his senses on an uneventful day.

He gave a startled yelp when a tomahawk bounced off a tree just beyond him with a wet thunk. With a silent curse, Sean MacLeod knew he was guilty of the deadly sin of revery. At the same time, he was thankful. A grown man sitting on a horse made a large target. Whoever threw that blade wasn't very good at it.

Hands sweeping for his rifle, he saw there would be no time to use it. Even though covered, he figured the powder would be wet anyway. The men rushing toward him along the narrow trail were too close. These were not Osage, nor any tribe he was familiar with. He didn't have to wonder why he was attacked. There was no time for that. His weapons and horse would be reason enough, a great prize for the taking.

A gentle tug on the reins caused Thunder to rear and slash at the men with his front hooves, while Sean slid off the back of the saddle to the ground holding his fighting knife. The maneuver bought him the time needed.

Rolling and dodging through the wet undergrowth, the two warriors evaded the horse, but Thunder had done his job. The Appaloosa was trained as a war horse and had been presented to him by old Bear Hunter of the Piikani, the Piegan Blackfoot. His vendetta with the Bloods was long over and the horse had served Sean well since.

From the first thrown tomahawk, he knew these men weren't here for polite conversation. No quarter would be asked nor given. Sean attacked the first man regaining the trail while he was off-balance, blocked his knife arm and brought his own fighting knife under the man's breastbone, leaving him bleeding out on the trail. The slain warrior was young and from the absence of scars, appeared untested. He would retain that in death. There were no second chances on the frontier.

The next warrior was another matter. Older, his chest and arms bore the scars of his education. He looked at his companion a moment while standing near-naked in the rain and then turned hate-filled eyes on Sean.

"You English?" The warrior's voice came as a guttural hiss filled with hatred.

The way he said English was a curse in any language. Sean was surprised the man spoke to him. That one word could mean a lot of different things. But it was not the time for a history lesson. There may have been an Englishman or two running around the woodpile of his lineage, probably being chased by Welsh warriors. Or the Danes, the French, the Germans, or who-the-hell cared at this point. But still....

Sean replied while checking the footing between them. "Close enough."

The man raised his tomahawk, and for a moment Sean tensed, thinking he would throw it. Dark, glittering eyes stared at him from a nearly hairless face. The scalp lock on his head was leaking red dye, and yellow coloring on his cheeks was about gone. It's hard to keep up decorations in the rain.

The warrior's voice was full of contempt. "English die today."

"It could happen." Sean shrugged, keeping a close watch on the man before pointing with his knife at him. "What tribe are you? Have I given you cause for this attack, some disrespect to your people?"

The warrior tapped the flat side of his tomahawk against his chest, his broken English hard to understand. "I am Shawnee and follow Black Hoof, the great prophet. You are White. You English. It is enough."

"I guess one reason is as good as another." Sean nodded, not knowing or caring who the prophet was the man followed. One man's quest was another man's reason to go fishing. The important part of the message was the tomahawk.

He shrugged. "Well, then. Goodbye...Shawnee."

There are few mistakes in the forest that don't result in death or injury, whether by animal or man. Struggles and fights to the death rarely take long. Most men aren't in any kind of shape for an extended fight and one of the adversaries is always better than the other or has a distinct advantage. Often the winner is decided on a simple mistake—an errant throw of a hatchet, a rock rolling under your foot, an off-balance swing leaving you defenseless, or underestimating an opponent...a matter of judgment.

When the man attacked with a shrieking war cry, the Spanish blade of Sean's fighting knife cut through the handle of the Shawnee's tomahawk, making it useless. With a shocked expression, the warrior paused and then dropped his piece of the handle into the grass. He grabbed for his knife, but it was too late. In one continuous movement, Sean was on him and quickly dispatched the man.

He stood over the slain warrior, getting his breathing under control, gaze searching the forest for any sign of more men. You never know who you might encounter in life. He firmly believed that no matter how good at something you are, there will always be someone better, a circumstance you can't fight your way through. Maybe just around the next bend. For these men in particular, a history lesson concerning the Ghostrider may have helped, if they'd had time to share stories over a communal fire. But probably not. There are always stories, embellished over time with re-telling. Sometimes Sean didn't believe his own memories. The fact remained. This was not his first battle.

Thunder's step was quiet as the horse moved up behind him, nudging his shoulder. He shook his head, scratching the horse between its ears. "Dunno, Thunder.

I don't know what this was about, and I've never seen a Shawnee before—I think they're an Eastern tribe." He paused to look around the forest. Why were these men here? If there were more, and he assumed there would be, where was the larger party?

This was not the way his day was supposed to go. Sometimes he yearned for the great mountains of the northwest where you could ride for days without meeting a soul. But he knew that dream was flawed. The land was filling up and growing. He had to grow with it.

Shawnee? Here? There were already too many tribes in this part of the country. A great migration was happening, caused by many factors—the influx of Whites east of the Big Muddy being one of them. Entire clans picked up and moved, seeking peace and fresh hunting grounds— encroaching on other tribes that claimed the land. It was a rare day when differing tribes could live next to one another.

That's the way it was at his destination, Jones Mill. Many tribes, none liking the other, barely keeping the peace. One more group arriving with strange customs wasn't a good thing.

In a short amount of time, the surrounding forest, darkened and shrouded with a steady, gray rain didn't look so inviting. It seemed to be waiting for something... something he didn't want to give. Something malevolent.

# Chapter Two

STONEFACE SAT RELAXED ON HIS HORSE, HIS BODY motionless as his name. They perched on a rocky hillside as the party of Whites navigated a trail below among limestone boulders overgrown with forest ivy and ringed with fern. Sunlight filtered through the canopy of trees. A light fog wound through the trees, chased into the shadows by the growing heat of the sun.

Alone on the hill, he knew any of the group below could see him if they looked. They would not. To look up and around—to see where you've been, along with where you're going, is a matter of training. These Whites moved as children in the forest with no thought of their surroundings except where to put their next step.

Two women rode in a sideways fashion atop their mules—movements stiff and working against the gait of the animals. They appeared awkward, not used to riding. One called to a man, laughing at his reply. The sun surrounded them in a misty halo and his loins stirred as he watched them. Pleasing, if you liked them skinny. His breathing quickened, picturing them splayed and bloody, begging for mercy he might offer but would never give. He eased himself on the blanket-saddle, gripping a red-streaked pipe-axe in one hand. The color on the handle was not paint, but the blood of his enemies.

Words of the old Shawnee chief Tenskwatawa echoed in his mind, telling his people to return to the old ways. The prophet Black Hoof assured them the spirits were not pleased with their children. Whites and Christians were a scourge to the tribes. They were guilty of witch-craft and caused the sickness of bleeding sores that killed his people. But the reckoning they yearned for by his people never came, the death of loved ones were never avenged.

Stoneface fought in the north country with the French against the incursion of the English. He then fought against his own appeasing people who thought tolerance was the way to peace and found himself branded a renegade. He was brutal against anyone who took on the yoke of Christianity, especially his own people. His actions failed to sway them, only making them turn away. Even the leaders he admired began to talk peace with the White man.

The press of tribes that were allied to traders and White settlers pushed him farther away from his home-land each year. Hoping to join forces with Black Hoof in a land called Kansas, he drifted south. His followers were like-minded. He chose his men for their size and brutal-ity. Their passage through the land was relentless, leaving a wake of death. There were no families with them. No women. They didn't carry much in the way of supplies. Those were collected and used along the way. Before any counterstrikes or reparations could be levied against them, they filtered away into the forest—always heading south, looking for the next victims.

The hardy souls who ventured far into the forest to live were often his victims. There was no communication between these far-flung settlers, no one to know of their passing except an occasional traveler. The isolated killings were easy, but that isolation didn't instill the fear he wanted because no one knew of it.

Drawing him from his thoughts, the sharp call of a crow came from the trees, and then two more on each side of the small caravan. It was time and his men were ready. He checked the group of people again. Not one person looked attentive at the calls of the crow. In a countryside that grows silent when men approach, why would they trust these sudden noises? Unbelievable.

A boy and girl followed the women on smaller horses. The men were on foot and scouted the trail ahead for the best way through the trees and rocks, strung out in a line that could not be defended. One carried a rifle slung over his back while looking at something held in his hand. How could these stupid Whites take over the country?

Earlier, Stoneface had tied a bit of red cloth to a bush. When the Whites reached that point it was time to strike. The first man walking point reached for the bit of red cloth, curious of its existence. Stoneface was surprised the man saw it. With his people in perfect position, Stoneface raised his pipe-axe for the signal, paused for a moment and then slashed downward through the air.

A fusillade of arrows and rifle balls erupted, and four men went down hard and didn't stir. The two remaining White men swept the women and children from the backs of their mules and pushed them toward cover. His braves rushed the last two men, overpowering and killing them in moments. It was quick and brutal, and meant to be. Not one shot was fired in return. There was no time.

The ambushes he orchestrated were always quick and overwhelming.

Stoneface walked through swirling powder smoke toward the women, with two warriors in front of him. The leading Indian laughed as a small boy rushed toward them with a knife. His laugh turned to a screech as his belly was opened with a vicious sweep of the blade. Avoiding the slashing blade, the other warrior dispatched the boy with a blow to the head. Crouching under a rocky overhang covered in ivy and branches, one of the women cried out in anguish, clutching the little girl to her breast as she watched them.

The other woman stood with no expression, hands clasped together and rigid in pose, staring into the forest. Stoneface gazed at her a moment and then shook his head. She didn't have a death song and would be no fun for them. Her spirit was already gone, leaving her an empty shell. He doubted she'd even feel the pain of violation. He'd seen men do this as well, when all was lost in battle, waiting for the hatchet or knife to end their life. Watching a moment, he smiled. The men could have her first. He wanted the woman clutching her daughter. She looked like a fighter.

Footfalls sounded from behind and he knew his men gathered. He motioned his axe forward and pointed toward the woman with the vacant stare. His warriors flowed around him like a slow-moving stream around a rock. They knew what to do. Screams would not carry far into the forest.

He advanced toward the other woman clutching her child. The little girl slumped against her mother, and then the lifeless body was lain gently aside. The woman stood defiant—blond hair wild in the morning light as she tried to bring the bloody knife to her own throat. But her act of defiance cost her. He was too quick, slapping her to the ground and stepping on the knife hand. And she fought—hard.

———

STONEFACE STRODE among the men as they gorged on the food supplies carried by the Whites. One warrior had a jug of whiskey. Stoneface grabbed it and smashed the pewter container on a rock. The last thing he needed was warriors drunk on the White man's devil water.

"Strip the bodies and leave them. When the Whites find these people, it will strike fear in their hearts and their legs will tremble. Load all the supplies on the mules."

"The boy? Must he be stripped?"

Big Hand was an Ottawa and his most trusted warrior. The man was ruthless in battle, but had lost children of his own and missed his old life. Stoneface would give him this concession. Though he'd not ordered it, the boy was the only one not cut by the knives of his men.

"Leave him with his knife in hand. Though a child, he was the only warrior among these people. What of the man he wounded?"

Big Hand shrugged, watching his leader with a flat stare. "He is holding his guts in with his hands."

Stoneface nodded. "Lone Elk thinks he has hidden the devil water he found. Give the wounded man the devil water to ease his pain and sing his death song with him. And then kill them both. We will find a place to hide the bodies. Nothing of us must be left here."

"Is all this needful?" Big Hand gave his leader a concerned glance. "We may make more enemies than we can handle, and Lone Elk has friends."

"I gave the order to destroy all the devil water. It must be obeyed." He looked at his second-in-command a moment. "The message brought to me from a man called Ambrose was to scare the people away from this land and there would be much gold for us. The gold would be left at a place called Jones Mill with few defenders. If we do this, we will have many of the White man's riches and much land for our people. We must move everyone out."

"What use do we have for their riches?"

Stoneface shrugged. "None, but they don't know that. And we shall have the land anyway. Our numbers will grow and we will rule. This Jones Mill will be our camp unless we find something better. Those who think we are controlled by them will be pleased—until we kill them too."

He nodded toward the wounded warrior. "Keep Lone Elk with you, along with another man. Once it's done, catch up with us."

His men bustled around, cleaning the area and packing all the plunder on the extra mules and horses. No sound came to his ears but the wind in the trees and the call of a distant hawk—the recent screaming and supplications of the woman was put away in a special corner of his mind. He would visit that memory later—many times. Nothing was left behind but the red-streaked bodies of the slain.

Stoneface raised his pipe-axe above his head, watching his men. Like a pack of wolves, every eye turned to him. Silent. Attentive. Feral.

"We go."

# Chapter Three

THE NEXT DAY AFTER THE ATTACK BY THE TWO Shawnee, Sean stopped his horse near the edge of a rocky bluff. Buzzards circled in the valley below. The thunderstorms of the morning had given way to afternoon sun and the broken clouds pushed toward the east on a steady breeze. Heat generated fog lingered in the valley below making it hard to count the number of birds weaving in and out of the rising mist. The number didn't matter. There were too many vultures in one place and that meant trouble.

He stood in the stirrups a moment to stretch his back. Sweat ran in rivulets down his body and his wet buckskins chafed him in places hard to reach. He could switch to cooler homespun clothing when he got back to Jones Mill, but that was a day away. Taking off his flat-crowned hat, he wiped his forehead with his sleeve before settling it back on his head. It was late August and he looked forward to the coolness of fall.

Thinking of Jones Mill brought his mind to Ellen Mackey, and he thought of her often. He'd rescued her from renegade slavers last year and they'd been together since. He wished things were better between them. She'd been distant lately and his thoughts of marriage were put away until he could figure out why. Lithe and quick, with dark hair and startling blue eyes, she was as good a hunter as he—sometimes better. But since her troubles a year ago, she seldom ventured into the forest. The fear in her was understandable but lasted longer than he thought it would.

They couldn't seem to hold a conversation, no matter the subject. When she criticized him over something or wanted to argue, he would walk away in anger. He liked to think a subject through before arguing. Truth was, he didn't like to argue at all. Someone once told him that you need to taste your thoughts a moment before you spit them out as words. Maybe that was the problem. He didn't have the skill to turn a quick phrase or hold witty conversation to delight a woman's ears or challenge her in verbal battle. She had enough of those skills for both. A woman can use words to cut a man's soul, and often does. That was never his way.

He was a warrior and hunter spending little time indoors. His preferred weapons were the fighting knife and tomahawk he wore and the English longbow he always carried. Late at night when the dreams came, he wished it were different. If he could be a shopkeeper like his adopted father or his good friend Shay, his life would be simpler. He yearned for that and remembered his early days as idyllic, until the Blackfoot forged him into a different man.

Thunder snorted his displeasure and took a step toward the shade at the side of the clearing. Sean reined him back a moment while he studied the forest below. He didn't blame the horse for wanting to get back into the trees and out of the sun. It was muggy hot after the rain.

There were dozens of buzzards circling below and they hadn't settled yet. The large number of the carrion birds meant there was a lot of something dead down there, far more than just the carcass of a dead deer or the remains of a bear that a hunter might leave. It seemed as if the birds were calling in reinforcements for the feast. The fact they hadn't settled to the ground meant there was something spooking them. The only thing a buzzard feared was man, and the black buzzards seemed to overcome that disposition.

He kneed Thunder toward the shade of a twisted pine, set close to the edge of the rocky bluff. His spyglass would be useless against the foliage below. Curiosity killed many a cat and frontiersman, but regardless of that, he started down a switchback trail that would bring him to the valley below. The trail was bordered by forest fern and lichen-covered rocks, too slick for comfort after the rain, and canopied by towering oak.

Thunder was a surefooted horse, so he let him pick his own way. When he slipped once on the wet shale, the metal horseshoes on his scrambling hooves rang in the stillness. Sean made sure his saddle-mounted pistols, smooth bore and filled with buckshot, were loose in their holsters. Anyone at the bottom of the trail would have heard the noise. But once started on this descent, there was no turning back.

His gaze searched the forest for any sign of hostility as he picked over his last thought. There was no turning back. How often does a man start on a trail with uncertain ending? Each day is a challenge with no promise of another. What lies beyond the bend in the trail or over the mountain is sometimes better left undiscovered. It was another piece of thoughtful advice given to himself and never taken.

They came to the bottom and eased into the mist-shrouded trees. The breeze carried the guttural cries of a few buzzards on the ground, and he turned his horse that way. The land around him contrasted with the dry plateau he'd left. He was still on a slope, surrounded with honeysuckle and deadfalls covered in moss and ivy. In the open spaces of the forest, tall grass brushed Thunder's belly and his hoof-falls were silent as they moved toward the sound of quarreling birds.

Sean paid more attention to the surrounding woods than where they were going. The horse tossed his head, and he felt the Appaloosa's skin ripple, then settle down. The horse moved forward with a nervous step, head up and alert.

He found the source of the carrion bird's attention in a small clearing, a natural cul-de-sac bordered by rocks and brush on three sides. A coyote slunk away through the grass as he approached, and then turned and watched —not wanting to leave an easy meal.

Several bodies lay stark white in a shaded and green background. Staying in dense cover, he waited a few minutes trying to figure out the story, and there was always a story. From the way the bodies were strung out it looked like the victims were on the move when the attack happened. They'd been dead only a few hours, judging by the small amount of damage by scavengers. He could assume the attackers were gone, but assumptions can get you killed. If they were gone, a larger question came to mind. What spooked the birds?

This was ambush country. No one does an ambush better, nor fears it more, than the Indian. Sean wasn't sure who'd done this deed. So far, he'd lean that way until he came up with a better answer. He counted a half dozen men, some with arrow wounds and a couple looked like they died of gunshots. The men lay along a faint trail leading around the bluff. It looked as if a couple of men survived the first volley and marshaled the women and children into an overhang of rock and vines to make a stand. Not a bad position if they'd had more time to prepare. But not against an overwhelming force.

He nudged Thunder forward and rode up to their improvised fort. What he saw inside made him turn his head a moment. He pushed down memories of losing his wife and son and turned his gaze back to this last desperate fight. One man lay belly down over a log, another sprawled on the ground. Behind them were the bodies of two women, a young boy and a girl.

Taking a final look around, listening for any discordant sound from the forest, he dismounted and ground-reined Thunder. Taking a deep breath, he steeled himself against the task at hand. Death wasn't anything new, especially in these wilderness foothills. But if you got used to it, you were already lost.

The long, flaxen hair of one of the women fluttered in a sudden gust of wind. The bodies of the women and the girl were thrown together at the foot of the overhang. Maybe they'd clung together, hoping and praying not to be killed. Part of their minds would argue death was better than being taken captive and sold, but more likely they'd hope for life. It was the only reason he could think of that they hadn't scattered and run. They'd been killed there, and then left where they lay.

The young girl was left with her clothes. The older women were naked, showing cuts and scratches as if animals had attacked them. Their final indignity was the loss of their breasts. He prayed they were dead when that happened, but from the amount of blood—doubted it. That blood loss alone would have killed them, along with the pain. He turned away, sickened by the sight and depravity. Seeing death was something he was used to. But this? No. Not this.

The earth was soft and he saw minimal signs of animal or vulture damage. It was too soon. They'd been attacked by the cruelest animal of all—man. He turned back and studied the ground. The earth was scuffed and in the last moments the women had fought, of that he was sure. There were smooth prints of moccasins and in the middle, on top of the others, a heel print of a boot. The print was defined and the edges hadn't filled in.

During the mutilation, or after?

Looking at the boy, he couldn't help but feel proud of him. Sean guessed he was eight or ten years old, and he'd come out to meet the enemy. Surely one of the women was his mother, possibly the girl his sister. He still had a knife gripped in his hand. That one object told him the boy had impressed his attackers. All the men he found were stripped of weapons, but the young man still had his knife. If it were Indians, he knew this was a sign of respect.

He kneeled by the young man and lay his hand on his shoulder, thinking of his own son who would never grow old. This young man proved himself even in death. He couldn't think of him as a boy any longer. If he had the words, he'd say a prayer. But prayer is for the living and too late for the dead—small comfort could be had at this point.

No prayer but a promise given. "I'll find them, boy. I'll find them and they will pay."

While he dragged the bodies together under the overhang, he looked for personal possessions thinking to see who they were but found nothing. Everything was taken except the knife. Part of the overhang was dirt and rock so after dragging all the bodies together, he collapsed that on top of them to make a burial site. He was sure he could find it again if anyone wanted. The larger question? Who were they and why were they here?

The area around the ambush site was a mixture of churned earth and trampled grass. All it told him was the attacking force was mounted and there were a lot of them. He still had no idea whether it was Indians, renegade Whites, or a combination of both. Still, he looked around for anything he could find. There was a new army detachment at Jones Mill and he supposed the man in charge would want to know. The arrows still in the men, broken when they failed to pull out, might indicate Indians. But he used arrows himself as did most of the hunters he knew.

He'd noticed an arrow point embedded in a tree, the shaft shattered on impact. Digging it out, he saw the arrowhead was made of flint. The arrows he used had iron points, shipped from England in bundles. His were longer to fit an English bow that was almost as tall as he. This was the only clue he had about the killers. Still, it didn't mean much. Anyone would pick up an arrow and reuse it, no matter the point.

There was nothing suitable for a grave marker, so he took an arrow and heated the point in a small fire, careful not to scorch and weaken the shaft. Once it was hot, he burned a message on a hard piece of buckskin he cut from his groundsheet.

*Unknown party of 10, killed August 1821.*

Cutting two holes in the marker, he threaded a stick through it and stuck it into the mass grave. He shook his head. It was a mystery and like most frontiersmen—he didn't like mysteries. Brushing dirt from his hands, he stood by Thunder and drank from his canteen. Finished, he rubbed the horse between the ears and fed him a dried apple from the stash in his saddlebag.

Catching a fine scent on a slight breeze, he walked toward a rock beside the trail. A brown pewter jug lay shattered at its base, the mouth of the jug still having a cork in it. Pulling it out, he brought it to his nose. It was rum, or a concoction called flip—but liquor, nonetheless. Someone had iron control of their men, not letting them drink. That was almost as unsettling as the murders. This was not a random act. And if this was not some ambush of opportunity, someone had a plan.

He looked around one more time. There was nothing more to be done. Once he left, nature would retake the area with no hint of the tragedy that took place in its cooling shade. He felt something profound should be said over the bodies, but the words did not come. It was time to go home and bring a warning of—what?

# Chapter Four

JONES MILL WAS BUILT AGAINST A BLUFF, ALONGSIDE A rushing tributary that flowed into the White River. The water source came from a huge spring that provided ice-cold water all year. When more settlers arrived, the mill was turned into a makeshift fort, with the buildings connected by their outside walls. With some expert advice from Indian friends, all the brush and trees were cleared away for the length of an arrow flight. Once that was done, grass began to grow in the sunlit meadow and was kept cropped short by grazing livestock.

It was a good location for keeping track of local movement of the different tribes found in the area, so a small detachment of soldiers resided there. They'd replenished their numbers after the defeat at the hands of renegades last year. It was like a strange play. The soldiers and Indians, especially the Osage, watched each other constantly. Woodsmen like Sean watched both with a jaundiced eye. Trouble was brewing.

Several people tended stock, fished or stood about.

They seemed to not have a care in the world. None were armed and he saw no sentries. He didn't think he'd been gone that long but didn't know any of them. New people must have moved in.

Sean sighed as he gigged Thunder in the flanks to get him to go into the cold water and approach the busy compound. Reporting the murder of the small party of people was on his mind and the commandant would be his first stop.

Riding through the small gate in the wall facing the river, he paused a moment. Voices singing a hymn carried through the windows of a building. He couldn't pick out Ellen's voice but knew she loved to sing. They didn't have a church. Some of the people took turns having meetings in their homes, or in good weather would meet outside.

"Must be Sunday."

Thunder twitched his ears but didn't care.

Knowing Ellen would be at the service, he guided his horse left and tied him to the hitch rail in front of the building that housed their small contingent of soldiers. He paused a moment to use his hat to slap dust and a few persistent stick-tights from his leggings, stalling a bit before he walked inside. Finally, knowing the task wouldn't get any easier, he moved through the door.

The first man he spotted was Lieutenant Ambrose, someone he didn't have much use for. When the soldier arrived months ago, they'd taken an instant dislike to each other. Ambrose was a martinet with his men and a popinjay to everyone who saw through his bluster. Unfortunately, Ellen wasn't one of those people. His hat was always carefully set on his head and uniform immaculate. His self-important manner and smooth talking influenced a few women around the settlement and Sean had heard whispers of some trouble because of that. Some of the rum-talk around the tavern speculated how the man would look as a gelding. Of greater interest was the polished riding boots the man always wore. Giving it little thought, he wondered if the heel marks at the massacre would match those boots.

Beyond him was an officer he'd never met. His plain uniform was unadorned with medals or ribbons and open at the collar. The buttons were simple wood. He couldn't tell his height, but his iron-gray hair put him in middle age. Since the man sat at the big desk, Sean assumed he was the new honcho and started that way.

Ambrose grabbed his arm. "Hold on a minute, MacLeod. You can't just barge in there without being invited. This is an Army post, not your rum-sotted tavern."

He stopped and looked at the lieutenant until the man released the grasp on his arm. "Lieutenant, you and I have had all the conversation we'll ever have. Don't touch me again."

The other officer rose at the sound of the altercation and motioned Sean to come inside. Giving Ambrose a smirk, he moved through the door, stopping in front of the desk. Glancing from him to Ambrose, the man eyed him up and down.

"And, just who are you that you would interrupt my" —the man glanced at his barren desktop with a small smile—"obviously busy day?"

Ambrose leaned through the doorway. "Colonel, this is the woods runner we've talked about. I'll get him out—"

"That will be all, Lieutenant. Please close the door."

Sean gave the lieutenant a small, mocking smile and

then turned back to the man in front of him. "I'm Sean MacLeod, and I've brought some bad news for you."

"Pleased to meet you, Mr. MacLeod. My name is Colonel James Thompson, and I'm about full-up on bad news. That's all I find around here. I arrived a few days ago and I'm still getting organized. But just because I'm new here, doesn't mean I'm inexperienced. You'll find"— he smiled at Sean—"I'm neither captain nor commander, so you'll have to leave that title to the lieutenant."

Sean liked the man already and started to smile until he remembered the news he had to share. "Colonel...."

The affable man stood and extended his hand. "Call me Jim and I'll call you Sean. Agreed? I've heard many things about the fabled Ghostrider—most of them good, of course. With one notable exception and you'll know who that is." He sat back in his chair. "I've met your lovely wife, Ellen. She comes in quite often to talk to Ambrose. Quite the lady."

Talking to that womanizer? "Really? That's odd that she comes here."

"Not for me to say." The colonel shrugged. "Now, what's the problem."

Sean studied the man a moment, hating to kill his mood. "All right, Jim. I came upon a party of ten people about a day's ride north of here. They were ambushed and killed."

The man became ashen and seemed to shrink in his chair, turned and stared out the window. Sean looked around for another chair, didn't find one, so he stood waiting.

Finally...in a voice rough with strain. "When I came here, part of my orders were to meet a surveying party and give them assistance to their duties. I believe that number would account for them."

The colonel turned to look at him, his face drawn into a haunted mask. He cleared his throat a couple of times before he could speak.

"This is hard for me. One of the women in the party was my daughter, along with her husband and two children. If there were hostiles around the women and children were supposed to stay here while the men surveyed the area. I don't know why they'd be...I can only assume it was them." He stopped another minute. "You say no survivors?"

He shrugged. "No, General. I didn't see sign of anyone getting away. The attack was too sudden and well executed."

"I'm not a...oh, I see. You have a strange sense of humor."

Sean reached across the desk and put his hand on the man's shoulder. "And, sometimes misplaced. It was your family and I'm sorry for that. For my part, I don't do well around people. My mouth gets away from me sometimes." He shrugged. "We can't help them. There's a lot of death in this part of the country. It's a dangerous place with many warring factions. Perhaps they didn't know that. I can't for the life of me fathom why they were traveling with no escort. That might be a question for Lieutenant Ambrose."

He sighed before he continued. "As for the humor, when death comes, we need to face up to it and spit in its eye. As a soldier, you know that. I'm just trying to lighten the load a little. Now instead of grieving for your family, you can be mad at me. I'm used to it."

The colonel straightened his back. "Did you bury them?"

"I did. But I can find the place if need be...I left a marker. They are covered but it's not a proper burial."

The man seemed to gather strength. "We'll fetch them back. Were they...?"

He looked at the man in empathy, knowing the pain he felt. "Jim, there's no point in putting yourself through this."

Misty eyes stared at him in a flat gaze from under bushy brows. He could almost believe the man's hair was turning grayer by the minute. His hoarse voice bore no semblance to someone used to command.

"I believe it's necessary."

Sean took a deep breath, trying to dispel some of his own demons. This killing hit too close to home. "I'm sorry for your loss. To be more specific, the men were stripped and mutilated. The women were...abused. It was brutal."

"The rest? Were they...?"

"Just the women and men. From what I could tell, the children were simply killed."

The colonel puffed his cheeks in a long sigh. "I guess it makes sense. My experience tells me the hostiles torture and mutilate everyone, given time."

Sean shook his head. The words expressed by the colonel were common and accounted for much of the hatred between Indian and Whites.

"Then you must have limited experience, sir. Most of the hostility here is generated by our meddling. That's the truth of it. Any killing done is usually a reprisal for something else, either some thoughtless action or the perception of insult. With few exceptions, the Cherokee are peaceful and God-fearing. The others? Not so much. Mutilation is not normal for the local Indians. I'm afraid there's more to this than we know."

There was a long silence before Sean finally broke it. "There is one other thing. At the last a few of the party holed up under an overhang to protect their back." He shrugged. "It didn't help much. I doubt they had but a few moments to find shelter or hide."

The man was staring off into the distance and Sean felt he was picturing it in his mind.

"Your grandson came out to meet the enemy and defend the women. I cannot imagine how afraid he must have been or the courage it took for a young boy to do that. With the number of the force facing him, he had to know it was hopeless. His only weapon was a skinning knife. All the men including his father, were dead or dying. I'm sure he saw that. I'd have been proud to call him my son and you should be proud of him too. He may have been a boy, but someone found out he was a man that day."

"He was ten years old." Wiping a hand down his face, the colonel's voice was strained. "How do you know this? Did you see it?"

Sean waited until the man calmed himself a little. "Any woodsman would tell the same tale. There was blood on his knife and his hands...and up his arms. It wasn't his. His wound was to the head, and I doubt he felt it. Before he died, he did some serious damage to someone. Think of it. The enemy comes running up and sees nothing standing in his way but a boy. I'm thinking at least one man got a surprise that took his life."

He shook his head. "They took all the weapons from the party, but they didn't take his knife. They gave him respect."

"Respect? That's little comfort. So, who is responsible? Indians? Renegades?"

"It's hard to tell. I lean toward Indians, but it could have been renegades like we had last year. And remember, there are renegades of every stripe—not just Indian.

They left nothing of themselves behind except a few broken arrows."

Sean cleared his throat. "The day before this happened, I was attacked by a couple of Shawnee warriors. I've never seen Shawnee in this area."

The colonel gave him a doubting look. "How'd you know they were Shawnee?"

"One of them told me." Sean shrugged. "He was quite arrogant about it."

Nodding, the colonel turned back to the window and bowed his head. His shoulders shook once, corded muscles trying to hold in the grief—and failing.

Sean took the bloodstained knife from his belt and lay it on the desk. "I don't know if this will help ease your mind. This is a simple tool, used by everyone. But today this knife is a symbol of a young man's courage. Hold on to that."

"If there's nothing else you need of me?" When no answer came, Sean stood at attention, though the man couldn't see it. "My sympathy, sir."

He turned and left the room, closing the door behind him as quiet as possible.

Ambrose was talking to a sergeant when he interrupted them. "Sergeant, no one goes into that room until called. No one. That includes this captain-commander."

At the sergeant's incredulous expression, Sean spoke to him in a soft voice. "Look, I just gave him some bad news. People were killed. Things were done. It's personal. He needs the time."

The sergeant looked at the door grim faced and then nodded to him. "I'll see to it."

When he glanced again at Lieutenant Ambrose, the man's face held a sick pallor as he stared at the closed door.

"Are you all right, Ambrose? You look like you've seen a ghost."

The man ignored him and walked away. Moments later, Sean stood outside the building, rubbing Thunder between the ears, his thoughts on a faraway place.

# Chapter Five

SEAN COULD STILL HEAR THE DRONING VOICE OF THE preacher speechifying and pontificating, so he headed for the trading post and Rob Shay's tavern. He was tired and for no other reason than having a bad morning. A few of the locals were standing around, probably waiting for their wives to get out of the meeting. It seemed an odd crowd for a Sunday morning. Maybe the preacher would have better attendance if he came to the flock, instead of making the flock come to him.

He plopped down on an upended barrel that was used for seating at the bar. "Shay, I'll have some of your coffee with a bit of rum sloshed in it. Please."

"I see you made it back alive." Shay was middle-aged gray, with a portly body and twinkling blue eyes. The scars on his knuckles and forearms were badges showing he wasn't a man to be pushed. "And you mean the same drink you always have? Like I wouldn't remember?"

"I doubt either of us has much control of what you remember, my friend."

Sean tried to put his conversation with the colonel

out of his mind. It was a quest doomed to failure. He thought to catch up on local gossip and have a cup of coffee before going to see Ellen. They'd talked of marriage, but not lately. Things were a bit strained between them and he didn't know why. The complexities of a woman's mind were far beyond his ability to figure out. Like most men, he'd admit to spending little time at that endeavor. Still...they were good friends no matter what.

He was anxious to tell her of the fertile land found to the north, where the prairie met the foothills in western Missouri. Maybe that would make a difference and bring some excitement—something for her to look forward to. After being gone a couple of weeks exploring, he was anxious to see her. He knew she'd be at the Sunday meeting a good while longer. That preacher could ramble on.

The purveyor of the divine word of God had wandered in a few months before, looking half-starved and well used. He rode a limping and spavined mule with a split hoof. His black coat was frayed at the edges with a bullet hole decorating the long tail. He wore a black wide-brimmed hat with a cut in the brim. The man and his message turned out to be as ambiguous as his name, Anais Thorne.

Sean listened to one sermon and figured out why someone gave him that bullet hole, and afterward changed the preacher's name to An-ass Thorne—the man did not appreciate it. It was a surprise that Ellen thought the preacher held the Word in the clutch of his hand. Sean didn't mind religion, just not the brand the preacher sold.

Leaning an elbow on the fitted and milled planks that passed for a bar, he peered at his drink. "Shay, did you ever notice the coffee you pour tries to jump out of the cup? Even the rum won't mix with it." He grimaced as he took another sip. "Boy, that'll kill the worms."

"That's why nobody drinks it. It's been sitting here since you left. If you'd ever finish what's in the pot, I could make some fresh." Shay held the coffee pot high and looked at the bottom. "I had to plug a couple of holes last week. Ate right through it."

"Now, I don't believe that. Whatever this is, it's too thick to run out the bottom."

Grinning, he looked up at his friend. "Well, I hear you got your wish. Missouri will be a state this month. You going to run for Congress now? I bet you've been giving speeches to anyone who'll listen."

Shay chuckled. "Maybe, but it's a little early for that. This country is spreading out, that's for sure. She'll be the 24th state. I guess that'll make some difference to places like Saint Louis, but not much to the folks out here. Not yet anyway. The good thing is we now have a government and rules to abide by. That's also the bad thing. If we can keep them from running roughshod over everyone, it'll be a miracle."

The man paused a moment to finish his cup of flip, a sweet concoction made of ale, rum, and molasses. Sean remembered drinking flip in Kawsmouth for the first and last time. It seemed a lifetime ago.

"Say," Shay continued. "Did you hear what that bullet maker is doing up north? Major Henry? He's outfitting a hundred men to leave from Saint Louis to explore the far western lands. Paying two hundred dollars in gold for the year. Some man named Ashley's going to lead them. I heard he's in the powder business, so I guess they'll have the corner on that market. That'll be something. The flyer I saw said everything is supplied to the men, plus they'll have money in the bank when they get back."

He jumped in while Shay paused to breathe. "They'll need every bit of powder and shot they can make, and then some. But they won't get very far west. Not without going north first."

His voice faded as he watched through the window. Lieutenant Ambrose marched toward the tavern, resplendent in dress uniform with polished brass buttons and regulation saber belted on his waist.

They'd lost the old captain-commander last year when he'd rode his men into an ambush set up by a French slaver they were chasing. When Ambrose first arrived at the post, Sean asked him why he dressed in his finery every day. The man told him it was to impress the native tribes with his authority. Sean thought maybe there were too many mirrors in the lieutenant's office.

Shay brought his mind back to their conversation. "Why can't they go west? They had that bunch that went with Captain Lewis and them twenty years ago. Gone a year and hardly lost a man. Surely they can do it again?"

"Maybe." Sean shook his head. "Twenty years is a long time and a lot can happen. The Arikarees are being pushed south by the Blackfoot. They either move or get slaughtered—men, women and children. They're holding ground west of Saint Louis and blaming Whites for all their trouble. They won't let anyone pass through without a fight. I heard from a trader that the Rees are plum mad right now. So are the Blackfoot to the north. The Rees are mad at the Blackfoot for burning their villages and killing everyone, and somehow mad at the Whites for letting it happen. The Blackfoot are mad... hell, they're always mad. A small party might sneak through their hunting grounds by being extra careful, but not a hundred men."

"Well, I don't see..." Shay was interrupted by the lieutenant.

"Mr. MacLeod." The man's tone was officious and abrupt.

Sean glanced at the man and then returned his attention to his friend.

"Aw, go ahead and talk to the man." Shay went back to polishing bottles. "That'll give me time to make up some more lies."

"While you're doing that, see if you can find me a hunk of bread or something. My belly's empty and that coffee is trying to start a revolution."

He turned to the soldier. "All right, Lieutenant. What's on your mind?"

The man fidgeted a moment with the top button of his collar. "Can we talk in private?" He gave Shay a pointed look.

"No, this is fine. Mr. Shay is my oldest friend and as such, knows all my dirty secrets. Speak your mind so I can get on home."

"Well. As you wish. There's no easy way to say this so I'll get right to it. A lot has happened since you've been gone these weeks on your scouting foray."

"Foray?" Sean rolled the word around in his mind a moment, and then turned to his friend behind the bar. "What's a foray?"

Shay scratched his chin. "Well, it's kinda...."

The lieutenant ignored the interruption. "Now that the surveying party is lost, the colonel may return to Fort Smith. I can't say as I blame him for that. There's nothing worth protecting around here. All the soldiers camped here will go with him. With no army present, the post will be unsafe and should be abandoned."

Shay looked up from the glass he was polishing. "You might be surprised at this, but we survived pretty well before you and your predecessor came and stirred up everyone." He glanced up, startled. The earlier comment caught up with him. "Surveying party?"

Sean nodded. "Found them a day north of here."

His friend sighed, looking out the window. "Dammit to hell. I watched them all ride out and wondered at the time why anyone would let them go without an escort." He gave Ambrose a pointed look, and then turned back. "Kids too?"

Sean nodded. "Kids too."

Shooting an irritated glance at both, the soldier continued. "As for me, when relieved of duty by the colonel, I'll be going to Saint Louis to serve until a new state capitol is set up."

"Well, that sounds really interesting." Sean glanced at the man and then turned away. "You might be surprised to learn that your intentions are of no great interest to me, Ambrose."

The man looked at the floor, and then back at Sean with a determined expression.

"When I leave, Ellen Mackey is going with me."

Sean's gaze snapped around and he studied the man a moment. He could no more process that information than if he'd just seen a whistle pig wearing a beaver hat driving a wagon. He'd been gone a couple of weeks scouting some land to the northwest for settlement. It was good, fertile prairie and he thought of moving there and setting up a store. Settlers would be coming soon enough to that country and would need provisions.

He gathered his thoughts and tried to concentrate on

what the man was telling him. The more he thought of it, the more he was convinced he misunderstood. Maybe he'd made a mistake by not going home first. Surely things hadn't changed that much in so short a time.

Keeping track of all the thoughts going through his mind was nearly impossible, there were too many. The main item, coupled with what the colonel had told him? What had been going on between Ellen and this man while he was gone?

"What in hell are you talking about, mister?" He looked over at Shay, whose mouth hung open and eyes bugged out like a stepped-on frog. "Shay, do you know anything about this?"

His friend tried to find his voice but couldn't, an occurrence equal to pigs flying or the Mississippi running backward. His valiant effort produced a few incoherent squeaks and finally, a head shake.

The lieutenant grabbed Sean's shoulder, pulled him around and smiled at him. "I know it's hard for a common woods runner to understand, but you must accept this. Things happened while you were gone. Often, matters of the heart happen quickly. Ellen and I have an understanding. You need to accept this. I'm taking her with me for safety, something that seems to be beyond your concern. She is not your wife, and you have no legal standing to prevent it. Furthermore, she has agreed to go. Informing you is merely a courtesy since you have no say in this."

He looked Sean's frame up and down. "I must say it continues to baffle me. What can you offer a woman like Ellen? She is beautiful and refined, a gentle woman. You? I mean, look at you."

A vision of Ellen the year before during the battle with renegades crossed his mind and he figured she'd killed more men in straight-up fights than this self-important asshat could ever dream of.

But being honest with himself he knew what the lieutenant saw—no bargain in looks, dirty and unkempt after two weeks out in the brush and he supposed he did need a shave and a bath. He was still in trail garb with buckskin leggings tucked into knee-length moccasins, a leather pullover shirt cinched with his belt holding his fighting knife in its metal sheath and possibles bag hung on the back. His powder horn and shot bag were still slung across Thunder's withers, along with his Hawkins rifle and a brace of pistols. And his bow. His English longbow was never far from his hand. His bloodstained clothing would have to be thrown out to be washed before Ellen would let him in the house—the blood coming from a deer he'd dressed out two days earlier.

Sean studiously finished his cup of coffee, grimacing as he looked over the rim at Shay—who still hadn't recovered his voice, and then turned to the soldier.

"Ambrose, we are not friends. That's no great revelation to anyone and I'm sure no loss to either of us. I don't know what's going on or what you're trying to achieve. Your petty schemes are not my concern. But you won't be taking anyone with you. Ellen made no mention of this before I left."

The lieutenant sighed and shook his head, glancing around at the stunned audience. "This is like dealing with a simple child. MacLeod it's of no consequence what you know or think. The matter is settled. I tried to do this the easy way, but it seems you won't listen to reason." He spoke to the wide-eyed Shay. "You're a witness. I tried to be reasonable."

He turned and back-handed Sean across the face. The muted sound of a glove against his face was eclipsed when Shay dropped the jug of rum he'd picked up. The crack of the pewter against the hard floor sounded like a shot, sending a few men scrambling for cover. The smell permeated the room, along with Shay's soft cursing.

After stepping back, and sharing an amused glance with the people watching, Ambrose continued. "Oh, I've heard of you and your famous fighting knife, and your revenge against the Blackfoot who killed your family. Not that I believe any of it. It's more likely you made it all up. Even if it's true, I can't imagine anyone bragging about success against a bunch of raggedy-tailed and unwashed tribesmen who know nothing of military tactics."

The man made a show of stretching to his full height. "I am a professional soldier. You should know I've been trained by some of the best swordsmen available, and I've killed men in battle. I feel obligated to tell you that. That's all I can do to save your life. Now, we can avoid any bloodshed if you hand over your weapons and let me escort you to the guardhouse. There is no shame in yielding to a superior man and the voice of reason. By the time you get out, we'll be gone, and this will all be a bad memory. You can go on about—" His hands waved aimlessly at the room. "—Whatever it is you do."

Sean hadn't moved, glancing between Shay and Ambrose. He was stunned, not by the slap but that he'd let the man do it. He'd seen it coming. On some level he must have deemed it harmless. He rubbed his jaw a moment. If that blow was supposed to be a show of strength, it was sorely lacking.

Sean forced himself to smile at Ambrose. "One thing you'd know if you ask around. I never brag. I leave that to self-important hollow-shelled popinjays like yourself." He held his hand up when Ambrose started to interrupt. "Now, please bear with me. I'm just a poor and uneducated woods runner, so help me out here. What if I don't let you arrest me?"

He spread his hands wide. "For my own safety and wellbeing, of course?"

"Of all the...?" The lieutenant stepped back. "You refuse?"

Shay tried to intervene, feet crunching on shards of pewter. "Sean. Don't."

Ignoring his friend, his gaze held the soldier's eyes as he shrugged. "I don't feel like being arrested today. I have things to do. Sorry."

"In that case you are formally challenged." Ambrose pulled his blade and stepped back again, bringing it straight up in salute and then pointing it at him. "You're going to the guardhouse whether you like it or not. I don't want to hurt you, but I will if you don't do as I say."

Sean almost laughed. The weapon wasn't a rapier with a thin and agile blade. The soldier wielded a heavy-bladed saber. Dangerous? Of course. It was fine in battle from horseback, hacking and chopping against men on foot and of course...pointing at things. But not very useful in close quarters.

The incongruity of the situation made him shake his head. He'd just traveled through Indian land for two weeks unscathed, well not counting the Shawnee. Now some idiot soldier was accosting him in a friendly bar. And he wasn't even drunk.

"I'm challenged? Formally? Like in a duel?" Sean smiled. "How very civilized of you. I've heard of them, but never did see one." He rubbed his hand over his face again, aware the gesture was becoming a habit. This situation was getting out of hand and needed to end. "I'll give you an alternative solution. Get the hell out of here and return to your detachment. Your challenge and insults are of no interest to me."

Shay tried again. "Lieutenant, you don't want to do this."

The man slashed the air between them with his blade and then stepped back, making a show of kicking a chair out of the way, silencing conversation in the room. His voice was loud so all could hear. "Arm yourself or submit to arrest."

Sean was still trying to figure out what was going on. If the man meant to confuse him and put him on defense, he'd succeeded. With a sigh he pulled his fighting knife, more as a precaution than anything else. The sound as it left the metal scabbard rang loud in a suddenly quiet room, a scabbard designed to sharpen the blade every time it was pulled. A curious thought came to him.

"Did you study basic tactics when your masters taught you the blade?" The soldier didn't answer. "Maybe they would have taught you the advantage the Romans had with their short swords against their opponents bigger, heavier blades? No? Well, they should have. Now, let's stop this foolishness before someone gets hurt. We can sit and talk about why you think Ellen wants to leave with you, or better yet...we'll wait and let her explain it. If you want to duel, you'll just have to do it with yourself."

Ambrose lunged forward with a shout. It was a decent move, but Sean was a veteran of too many battles to be fooled. He stepped to the side and the saber slid along his buckskin shirt right under his armpit. Before the lieutenant could withdraw, Sean stepped forward and trapped the man's sword arm against his body.

Their faces were close together as he spoke in a soft voice. "Last chance to stop this, Lieutenant."

Startled, Ambrose jumped backward, a look of disbelief on his face. He attacked again, and Sean gave way before the longer weapon. He waited for an advantage, dodging and turning until his hips hit a table behind him. Sliding to the side, he parried another blow and then the men came together in a clinch. He knew Ambrose was weak as soon as they grappled and with a twist of his wrist the saber clattered to the floor. He started to step back.

"All right, Lieutenant, you made a good try so...."

Almost too late, he saw the dagger filling the man's other hand and streaking for his belly. Startled, he twisted away and the dagger sliced upward across his chest. Almost of its own volition, his own blade followed and Ambrose took the blow with a grunt. The lieutenant's breath expelled onto Sean's cheek as they held each other in a near embrace—and then the strength left Ambrose's legs and he was on the floor, bleeding out. One leg drew up as if he were going to try to rise, but then he settled onto the sawdust.

# Chapter Six

SEAN LOOKED UP AT HIS FRIEND BEHIND THE BAR. "I didn't want this."

"I'd testify to that." Shay peeked over the counter at the body. "Maybe it was the coffee."

A gasp came from behind him and Sean turned to see Ellen standing in the opening of the door, hair highlighted by the bright light behind her. She wore a long-sleeved blue gingham dress with a white collar—her best go-to-meeting dress, and he felt a momentary regret that he didn't provide better for her. Taking another deep breath, her fingers crumpled the starched bonnet she'd taken off to come inside.

When her eyes adjusted to the light in the room she walked forward through the sparse crowd with measured cadence as people scrambled to get out of her way, her gaze never leaving the body on the floor. She stood with one hand over her mouth, slowly shaking her head before lifting her gaze to his. The bonnet dropped unnoticed to the bloodstained sawdust; the ribbons used for ties trailing through her fingers.

"I heard you were back. Anais saw you ride through during the service." She moved her gaze back to the lieutenant's body. "What happened, Sean? Why do you always have to kill? He was a good man. Will you never stop?"

Her words hit him as a body blow. It put a knife in him and left a wound he felt would never heal. Was it true? Did she have feelings for this man? Anger pushed his reply.

"You didn't seem to mind my killing ways, as you call them, when I took you from the renegades last year. Maybe you'd rather have stayed?" He searched her eyes, waiting for an answer that didn't come. Finally...quietly, he asked her the most important question, at least to him.

"When were you going to tell me?" He stood before her in anguish, weakened knees barely holding up his mantle of sadness. His blade dripped blood on the wood shavings that covered the floor—blood that just missed draining from his own heart.

For the first time she looked hesitant and wouldn't meet his gaze. "This isn't the place to discuss this."

He looked around the room seeing a full range of expressions from anger to calm acceptance and indifference on the faces around them. Settlers and soldiers were present, along with a couple of Cherokee women who helped Shay tend the sturdy wooden tables. Some of the faces were new to him. Jones Mill was a growing community, and the room was filling with more people every minute. News travels fast and many of the settlers were present because they'd been at the Sabbath meeting.

"Ellen, I just killed your lover in front of these people. They'll be the judge concerning what I've done and why it happened. I'd want no other to be my jury of peers. Besides, your man gave me little choice."

His left hand held his side. Bright with blood, he stepped forward and wiped it down the front of her dress and she gasped at the intimate contact. He couldn't keep the bitterness from his voice.

"A little remembrance for you. He came close to solving all your problems."

She looked down at herself, shook her head and seemed to come out of a trance. "He wasn't my lover. Please, don't think that. He was not." She looked at the people congregated around them. The makeshift jury of their peers watched with avid interest. "You all know me and see me every day. Nothing like that happened. I did mention wanting to go to Saint Louis and he offered to take me. That's all."

He kept pressing her. "You had time enough to talk about leaving and to make plans with your man, but no time to talk to me about it?"

She stomped her foot on the floor and he almost smiled. Some things never change.

"I couldn't talk to you because you were gone." Her voice rose, strident with emotion. "And he's *not* my man."

Shay spoke up. "Ambrose painted an entirely different picture than that, Ellen. He goaded Sean to fight and then challenged him, struck him, and then threatened arrest. I'm thinking he wanted Sean out of the way for something."

Ellen shook her head. "Then he didn't know my Sean—"

"—Your Sean?" His gaze pinned her.

They were interrupted by one of the soldiers coming forward, hat in hand. "Pardon me, folks. This is interesting and all, but we've got a job to do. Let me get the lieutenant out of your way and over to the livery. We'll get him buried." He paused and looked around at the ring of onlookers. "I saw it all and there's no fault here for Mister MacLeod. Lieutenant Ambrose started this and exercised bad judgment in pushing it to his own end. I'll put that in my report to the colonel."

The man shook his head before clamping his hat back in place. "I don't know what the high muckety-mucks at Fort Smith, or the building across the way will think about it. The officer corps don't think much of enlisted men or their opinions. And they sure don't think much of their brother officers being killed." He tipped his hat with that statement and the blue-coated soldiers took their lieutenant out into the bright morning light.

Taking away the body seemed to break the attention of everyone. Men wandered out the door, some just turned to their tables with the Cherokee women doing a brisk business in flip and straight rum. Starting this early, Sean was sure most would regret the early drinking by nightfall.

Shay came around the bar with a clean white cloth for a bandage. "You're making a puddle on my floor."

"Here, give me that." Ellen grabbed the bandage and motioned for Sean to lift his shirt. "Seems my dress is already ruined."

She gave him a pointed look. "My *best* dress."

The wound was a shallow gash along his side that bled a lot but wasn't serious unless it became infected. With him holding his shirt up, he was a captive audience and she took full advantage.

Her voice was fierce, while whisper soft in desperation. "Please listen to me. We've been together over a year since you rescued me and helped find Beth. You've treated me well and Beth considers you a father she never had. For that alone, I owe you more than I can ever repay. Between you and Buffalo Shield, you've given Beth a feeling of self-worth she's never had before. It's something I could never give her, and I am grateful."

"Even if all that is true," he said. "You gave me more."

Tears ran down her face. He still couldn't stand to see that. As his hand moved to wipe away the tears, he strained to hear her voice.

"I'm confused, Sean. We've had a good run, but maybe it's not meant to be. I'm scared to death of another attack like the one we had three weeks ago. We were able to fight them off, but how long can we keep doing that? One of these days they'll break through. What then?" She looked up at him. "What then, Sean? I'm scared."

He knew what she meant. Her capture and rape years ago, and then being captured again last year along with her daughter, preyed on her mind. They had talked about it. She was such a strong woman, maybe he discounted her fear. And then three weeks ago the post was attacked in an early morning raid by a mixed band of warriors. He saw Osage, Delaware and a couple of men—hell, he had no idea where they'd come from. It was lucky one of the settlers was out hunting ducks at dawn and saw them coming. The Indians weren't too dedicated to the attack because they left after a few casualties. He figured they were mostly drunk.

Right after the attack, and after much arguing, they'd sent Ellen's daughter on a journey to Saint Louis for schooling. Ellen wanted no chance of her daughter being captured again or subjected to the same things she'd endured. He didn't agree but couldn't blame her. It was a stroke of luck that a large party of trappers that Sean knew and trusted were going north, so they sent Beth with them along with a letter to Chouteau's Post enabling her to use Sean's money to pay for her room and board. It would take her a month to get there, but they felt she'd be safe on the journey. It was a short notice plan and both he and Beth had been overruled by a determined Ellen. He still didn't like it.

As the party of men left, and after threatening to tie Beth on her horse, the old Blackfoot medicine man Buffalo Shield came to see him. Their friendship had a rocky start and wouldn't have happened at all except for Beth.

"It is time for me to go to my homeland. I will make sure the small one has a safe journey, and then I will return to the land of my fathers." He put his hand on Sean's shoulder. "To send her away is a wise choice. I have told her this. All the tribes are angry. They have much hatred for each other. Being pushed here by the Whites does not help. It is a bad time." The old man paused a moment. "I am old and have forgotten many things. One thing I know. You cannot always control the things around you. Sometimes you just have to go where the spirits lead. Your spirit is strong, Ghostrider. Follow it. Do not fight against it."

Sean nodded his agreement to him, although he wasn't sure what the Indian was talking about. He knew the real reason for his departure was to see Beth to safety and figured he'd follow her all the way, maybe even stay. The old Indian had adopted her as soon as the wily young lady called him grandfather.

He clasped the man's shoulder. "I will miss you, old friend. Safe journey."

———

THINKING about that didn't help with his anger toward Ellen. He felt like a dog worrying a bone. "So, now things are starting to add up. Even Buffalo Shield knew you would be leaving?"

Startled, she glanced up at him. "I don't know how. But I talked to Beth about it and she talks to him. I didn't keep it a secret."

He gave an exasperated sigh. "You kept it from me good enough."

"Dammit, you're never here. You're always out hunting, or scouting, or...or something." She put her hand on his arm, speaking softly and trying to draw him to her. "Look. We aren't married. The passion we felt in the heat of battle has faded."

"For you, maybe. The last time we were together that flame burned damned hot as I recall."

Her face flushed and she glanced around to see if anyone was listening. "Don't do that. There will never be a day that I don't think of you." She shook her head, wringing her hands. "Please try to understand. We were thrown together and everyone thought we should be a couple. You know all this. Don't try to fix something that doesn't need it. I'm sorry it worked out this way. And don't worry about me or my reputation. Folks can't think any less of me than they do now. It's not like I was some naïve virgin when we met."

Bitterness spilled over as she wiped away a tear coursing its way down her cheek. "All those pious women going to church service and looking down their noses at me still want to know how it feels to be captured and raped—they want all the little details. You should see them trying to hide their flushed faces behind fans and hats. I tell them if they're so damned curious, then go find out for themselves."

"None of that was your fault. Anyone that matters will know that." He watched her eyes fill with tears again and felt helpless before it—helpless before everything that was happening.

Ellen's voice turned cold and the tone surprised him. "People didn't like that I'd been captured and had a half-breed child and they sure didn't approve of you and I living together, although when no preacher is available it's done all the time. I think it will be easier to live where no one knows me." She glanced at him and then shook his arm. "Are you listening to me?"

Once again, he gazed out the window. Energy drained from him like water leaving his body and he couldn't seem to stop it. Looking over the head of Thunder, his Appaloosa war horse standing hipshot by the hitch rail, the wind swirled the tops of the trees and he could hear a thunderstorm growling in the distance, going away. Like her. He couldn't stop the storm and he couldn't stop her. He shivered under her touch.

His mind jumped to the memory of a twister he'd seen. Everything around him had been calm, but in the distance the giant wind sucked everything it touched into a black cloud surrounded by lightning—never to return. He was helpless and afraid then, and helpless now. This was a battle of the heart, not of cold steel and blood. It was a fight he wasn't prepared to wage and in fact, had already lost. He guessed Buffalo Shield was right.

He tried one more time, in his mind the last time. "We have a preacher. An-ass can marry us."

She stood mute for a moment, tears running down her cheeks. "Now? Now you want to get married? Damn you, Sean MacLeod."

He hung his head and sighed. Like trying to draw air

through a water-soaked blanket, the effort to breathe was tiring. "I'll get my things out of your cabin today."

"It's not..." She put her hand on his cheek, trying to get him to look at her. The warmth of her touch had always been a comfort and he leaned into it a moment.

"Sean, please. You don't have to do that. I have to make other plans now, and it may be a while before I can leave. Stay with me and you can have the cabin after I'm gone."

Stay with her? She was running hot and cold. He was too tired to keep up. His mind was full of confused and jumbled pictures of their time together. Maybe he could persuade her to stay. Maybe if he loved her enough...he shook his head, willing himself to meet her gaze.

"No. That's a pain I can't endure and I'd be a fool to try. It's best if I go. You made up your mind without talking to me, without giving me a chance. If I hadn't returned in time, it's a safe bet you'd have left without saying goodbye."

She tried to argue but he held up his hand. "Say what you will, but you didn't trust me. You gave that trust to someone else. I don't know what else to do, except leave. I gave you all I had, all I knew how to give, but I guess it wasn't enough." He drew his hands over his face, seeking energy he couldn't find.

"Beth has my letter of credit with the Chouteau's in Saint Louis. It's a goodly sum and I want you both to have it. If you share that money, you'll be well taken care of for a good while. I hope you find what, or who, you're looking for. My hope is you'll recognize what makes you happy when it's in front of you. Have a safe journey, Ellen."

She stepped in front of him as he tried to walk away, eyes flashing in anger. "I know that terrible male pride of yours believes there was someone else—that the only possible reason I'd leave you is for another man. As God is my witness, there is not. I'm not looking for anything except to be with my daughter and lead a safe life where I don't have to worry about being killed or captured. When your arms are wrapped around me I feel safe, but when you're gone...?" She shook her head. "Can you at least understand that?"

"So, to make you feel safe, whose arms were wrapped around you while I was gone?"

The thought and comment came unbidden, and his face turned sharply from the force of the slap. He saw it coming—gave it to her as her due. Getting slapped seemed to be a trend for the day. This one hurt the most.

He ignored her hot stare. His mind was on raucous Saint Louis and all the stories he heard from merchants and trappers. It was hardly a place for any decent woman to live. And yet, she'd sent Beth there for schooling. He still didn't like it.

Shaking his head, he continued. "If you think all predators wear buckskins, you're mistaken. I'm thinking they just carried one of them out the door."

She took a deep breath, controlling her anger. "That kind of danger I can handle. I have my blade and you taught me a lot in the last year." Her eyes filled with tears again. "I am sorry, Sean. I think my journey is set and I know the way. But your journey is still before you, and I can't help."

He couldn't stop the words. "I don't know what you think my journey is supposed to be. I thought it was over when I found you. But if there must be a journey, I can think of a better way to start than by having my heart cut out by someone I love."

Tears coursed down her cheeks as she turned away and mumbled something.

In that moment he noticed everyone had given them wide berth. The room was empty except for Shay studiously polishing the same glass he'd started a lifetime ago. Sean caught her and bowed his head close to hers and asked her to repeat what she'd said. They'd shared a lot in the last year, but her words took him in the belly—white hot, unexpected and painful.

Her breath came warm to his ear and made him think of better times. Until her anguished whisper gutted him.

"You call her name in your sleep. I can't compete with that. I don't know how."

# Chapter Seven

SEAN STARED AT ELLEN AS SHE WALKED AWAY. SHE looked defeated and he felt the same way. His shoulders slumped and he stood with head bowed.

She was right to get away from him and deep-down Sean knew it. The knowledge didn't make it any less bitter. But the dreams were starting again and several times he'd awakened in the middle of the night sweating and standing outside their cabin—with no idea how he got there. It was no better on the trail.

It was always the same. Dreams of night battle with fire all around, warriors running—wailing and screaming. The dreams started after Angie and little Angus were massacred by the Blackfoot and he knew he called to them in his dreams—wanting to save them. During his vendetta with the Bloods, he dreamed of them every time he slept.

He gave a long sigh, glancing around the post. It was defensible...to a point. Against an overwhelming force? Never. The peaceful year was at an end. Now, the call of battle coursed through his veins again and he didn't know why. Was Ambrose a victim of this? Could Sean have walked away? Should he have?

He didn't want this now, but he couldn't ignore it. There was only one reason for the dreams to start again.

Something was coming.

————

SEAN STOOD on the landing in front of the trading post with Rob Shay. Ellen's cabin made the northernmost point of the stockade, and she sat on the front porch in her rocker. He'd bought it from a trader out of Fort Smith and she loved it. He sighed and watched her shoulders shake as she cried.

"Go talk to her, Sean. Maybe you can fix this. She's a good woman. You know that."

He looked at his friend and shook his head. "Nope. If there's anything I've learned over the last year it's that once she's made up her mind, it's set. Maybe her feelings will change, and I'd welcome that...but it won't be anytime soon. She wants to be with Beth and away from me. Can't say as I blame her. When I think on it, I'm surprised she didn't leave with the girl weeks ago."

"Maybe she was trying to decide what to do about you. Too bad. I thought you had something...together, I mean."

Sean nodded. "The sad thing? I would have stayed. When I left to look at that land up north, she never said a word. If she'd spoke against it, I would have stayed."

He thought about the last year and the events that led up to it. They'd been thrown together in a whirlwind of battle. There'd been physical attraction—no doubt about it. At the end, after the rescue, it was expected for them to stay together. Hell, everyone pushed them together including her daughter, Beth. His thoughts came back to Shay's last words.

"Yeah, I thought we had something too. Guess she doesn't. But either way, she's got to work it out and her going to Saint Louis means she wants to do it alone."

"Still...." Shay lifted a shoulder and then shook his head. "I couldn't help but overhear. If she thinks the problem is yours, and you think it's hers, how will you ever reach a balance?"

He looked at his friend a long moment. "I don't know...I really don't. She wants me to go where I can't. I want her to stay where she won't. Fear is eating at her and I can't seem to help. I'm thinking there's no good ending to this. If it's possible, take care of her for me. See she gets where she wants to go."

"Of course we will." Shay looked around at the building behind them. "This place is about worn out. I'm looking at the peeling logs on the wall and the overhang that needs repair. My last set of glass windows were shot out weeks ago. Waxed paper doesn't let in much light and flies stick to it."

He shook his head, shrugged and seemed to come to a decision. "We'll see she gets there safe. I've a mind that me and the wife will go with her. We've talked about it. I'm getting old and that soldier-boy was right, at least somewhat. If the Army leaves things will get a might interesting. There's an ill wind blowing hereabouts. I keep hearing rumors of the government relocating all the tribes—officially, I mean. Hell, they've been migrating west for years. There will be trouble."

Shay continued. "We'd like a chance to enjoy life a

little, and this may not be the place. When the Osage come back for the winter and see all the people on land they claim for hunting, it could get messy."

Sean knew what he meant. And it wasn't just in his friend's mind. Trouble was coming. And any trouble with the tribes usually came in the summer when food was plentiful.

The hot wind hissed through the tops of the pines. If heard at night, you'd shiver and think of storms—or conjure up a ghost or two.

"You're a good man and a good friend, Shay. You've done well with the post." He poked the man in the ribs. "Don't enjoy life too much in the big city. Your wife will put a knot on your head."

"That's a true statement." Shay ruefully rubbed his head at the thought. "So, what will you do?"

Sean looked around one more time, his gaze finally settling on Ellen's front porch. The empty chair still rocked, aided by the strong breeze. No good ending. Not here.

He didn't need much. A good woman. Hearth and home. Hunting and fishing to provide for his family. Life should be simple. Those things he could understand. And now? He was ill-equipped for mind games—and it was no game. He had all the information available, but knowledge of what to do with it trickled through his fingers.

"You still have some of those little black powder horn sticks we used to blow out tree stumps this spring?"

"Yeah, but what're you going to do with dynamite?" Shay looked closely at his friend and then at Ellen's cabin. "Let's not add stupidity to your other troubles."

Sean looked toward the forest, remembering a Cherokee friend he'd passed early this morning riding to the post. Red Eagle was a man who stood by him when he needed it. Their clan was putting together a fish camp as he rode by.

"Why, Shay, I'm going to do what any man with woman trouble does. It's a time-honored tradition. I'm going fishing."

# Chapter Eight

Jim Walker stepped off the barge that brought him across the Missouri River, leading a frazzled sorrel gelding with an arrow wound in its rump. He stopped to rub the horse between its ears, and then led him up toward Chouteau's trading post. The horse had carried him through scrapes with Blackfoot and lately the Arikarees. He still had to run his hand through his hair to believe he'd not lost his scalp. Every Indian he'd met, and most of the trappers, seemed to be mad about something, at war with someone.

Even the animals were mad. He'd had a bear chase him for a mile. Of course, that was not new for man or animal. All the tribes fought for territory as their numbers grew and they didn't want to share with the trappers and settlers moving into their country. And the bear? Who the hell knew? Probably went to sleep on an ant nest and woke up cranky.

The first stop was the livery with instructions to care for the horse and its wounds.

"Don't ya have a pack animal?" The hostler gave him a curious glance.

"Sure I do," Jim said. "The Arikarees are holding it for me...promised to take real good care of it. I'll make you a deal. You can have the mule and the pack that was on it if you want to go get it."

"Naw." The hostler shrugged, shooting him a sly grin. "They prob'ly et the mule and yer traps are too rusty to use."

"Yeah, well I still have my hair...at least most of it."

His belly was asking if his throat had been cut, so his second stop was the eating hall to see if he could rustle up some food. A few men loitered at the long, plank table. Not much had changed since he'd been here with Sean MacLeod in the past. A young woman dressed in a white linen dress came out and stared at him.

"What are *you* doing here?"

Surprised at the outburst, he looked around the interior of the building. Sure enough, there were plates of food and drinks in front of the other patrons. The woman was Indian, but he couldn't tell what tribe. He couldn't understand her attitude. He didn't have a bad reputation, although there were some that might argue with that.

"Like the rest of these men," he said cautiously while making sure he just straddled the bench so he could escape if need be. "I'd like a bite to eat if it's not too much trouble. I can pay extra, if you want."

She stared at him a moment, nodded and left. Watching her leave, he looked around again, scratching his head. That was...strange.

There was no chance to relax on the trail, not if you want to keep your hair. It was relatively safe in the dining hall. Relative because, from the woman's attitude, he wasn't sure she'd come back with food or a scalping knife. Tiredness settled in his bones and muscles as he leaned his elbows on the table, cradling his head. His gaze blinked lazily around the room, senses lulled by the steady drone of conversation. The only thing keeping him awake was the growling in his belly.

A nudge on his shoulder startled him, not realizing he'd fallen asleep. He glanced up and memories washed over him.

The last time he'd visited Chouteau's Post he'd met Sean MacLeod. They'd crossed the river in the company of a nefarious ferry boat owner named McGarry. They'd watched each other's back and prevented them being robbed blind or killed, striking up a friendship in the process. Before Sean left to head south, they enjoyed the companionship of a mother and daughter combination that left them both a little frazzled and confused. It was not normal for that to happen. The ladies Nez Percé grandfather had been impressed with Sean's Appaloosa warhorse, something the Nez Percé were known far and wide for raising and training.

Walker shook his head to clear his thoughts. "Fawn? I wondered if you'd still be here. How are you?"

The woman didn't speak for a moment, her expressionless eyes looking him over. Slight of build like her daughter Willow, she'd filled out, becoming even more attractive.

"So, you have decided to return?" She sat on the bench facing him. "Much has happened since you were here last, but I am as well as I can be."

"Good." He still couldn't decide on her expression. "Maybe we can still be friends?"

Shrugging, he saw a ghost of a tear trickle down her

face. A ghost because she immediately wiped it away with an angry swipe of her hand.

"When you and your friend were here, you left us with many memories."

He nodded, smiling at those memories and a little disconcerted with her gaze boring into his eyes. They'd had a good time, but....

"Are you a man, Walker?"

He gave her a quizzical look. Where was this going? "Well that's obvious, isn't it?"

Fawn nodded, giving a small smile. "I have much reason to know you are male. But are you a man, a man that takes responsibility for his actions?"

"I try to." He gave her a wary glance, trying to scoot away from her on the bench. "I'm not sure I like where this is heading, Fawn. What's going on?"

She stood and pulled at his arm. "Come with me."

"Well..." His stomach grumbled again.

Pulling him away from the table, she slapped his stomach. "We will take care of this in a few minutes."

"I ain't sure I got that long. I've been riding a pretty hungry trail lately."

They moved down the hallway and she stepped into a familiar room. He stopped at the threshold, boots skidding on the wooden, polished floor.

The woman he'd first seen when he came in sat on a narrow, hard-looking bed with two small children, both around a year old. One was a girl, already with a full head of black hair and brown eyes that seemed to stare intently at him, and then at Fawn. But the boy...

"Great jumpin' jehosaphat! How...?" Dressed in soft buckskin shirts and moccasins, they were sharing a few toys between them while chewing on pieces of dried apple. Their features were similar enough to make them brother and sister—except the boy was blue-eyed, and what hair he had was showing up white-blond on a dark-complexioned face.

"How?" Fawn stared at him and then made a circle with the fingers of one hand while poking the index finger of her other hand through the circle, moving them back and forth. "You have forgotten?"

No, not forgotten. Dreamed of...he did some numbers in his head. And possible. "The girl is yours?"

She watched him expectantly. "Ours. She is part of the memory you left."

"I thought you were past the age of worrying about having babies." He was slowly shaking his head trying to come to grips with everything.

Fawn gave him the first real smile of the day. "Me too. It would seem I was wrong."

"Well, hell." He drew his hand over his face. "Although I think the answer is obvious, who fathered the boy?"

She nodded assent. "Ghostrider."

The other woman moved quietly out the door and Fawn sat on the bed. Both children climbed on her lap and began pawing at her breasts. She pulled open her top from the sides exposing her breasts and the kids immediately latched on. Her expression softened as she watched them a moment and then looked up at him.

Jim voiced his confusion. "The boy's mother—your daughter...I don't remember her name. Why isn't she...?"

"Willow is dead." Fawn interrupted and then motioned to a bench sitting against the wall. "Sit. I have a story to tell."

Pulling the bench out from the wall, he plunked down with a sigh. "No doubt about it."

Nodding toward the suckling kids, he smiled at her. "That's distracting."

She moved, trying to get more comfortable. "Why?"

His stare was vacant a moment as he thought back over the last couple of years. This woman was the last he'd been with. He shrugged and smiled. "Because I did not forget."

She raised the girl a little. "Neither did I."

He relaxed, giving up on having a meal anytime soon. It wouldn't be the first time he'd gone hungry. "So? The story?"

"Willow was Nez Percé, as am I. Our bloodline is very important to our tribe. She was married to a jealous warrior but there were no children. Grandfather came up with the plan that she would lay with Ghostrider to make a child. As you can see, the plan worked."

He nodded, remembering how things happened. "Yeah, but...?"

She nodded. "When her husband saw the baby, he was angry. He kicked her in the stomach. It was too soon after the birthing and she started bleeding. She died. When Grandfather tried to help, he was killed. This angered our clan and Willow's husband was also killed. Both sides had many friends and there was a battle between the clans—many were killed. I ran away with the babies."

"Must have been one hell of a family reunion."

She nodded. "It was lucky that I'd given birth a week before, so I could nurse them both."

"How did the clan take to your being with child."

She shrugged. "I'm no longer welcome. Chouteau lets me stay if I work for him in the kitchen. It's a good thing you have come. He wants me to do other things I do not want to do, like laying with men for money. I refused but he keeps pressing, threatening to put us out."

Jim sat with his head in his hands, trying to order things in his mind. He'd deal with Chouteau first thing. If women did this of their own free will, that was fine with him and the way of the world. Forced prostitution was another matter, although prevalent in some places.

Her first question came back to him. Are you a man? He glanced up and found her watching him with an intent gaze, waiting him out. It didn't take much to realize how much his decision would mean to her. He sighed and nodded. Her expression softened again, and he thought she looked relieved.

"Will you take your daughter and lay her down? They're both asleep."

He couldn't remember ever holding a small child. She was still latched when he took her, and Fawn flinched as her nipple popped out. Holding the girl to him a moment, his gaze sought out Fawn's.

"Looks like I'm going to take up tepee living."

Her intake of breath was sharp. "You don't...I don't expect that. Most men would leave. It happens all the time. All I hoped for is help getting away, maybe some money for supplies—a place to live."

"I'm not most men. Besides, I'm tired of dodging hostiles for a few beaver pelts and combing arrows out of my hair. Every place I go people are mad about something. There's got to be a better way of making a living."

"What of this one?" She lay the boy down next to the girl, eyes soft as she caressed his head. Although the same age, the boy was already much larger than the girl. "Will you take him too?"

"Well." He grinned at her, having just come up with a plan. "I could, no question about it. But what we're going to do is take him to see his papa. I've kept track of him and heard he's at a place called Jones Mill, a few days travel south of here."

She looked doubtful. "Will he be pleased?"

He laughed and then shrugged, hoping he didn't wake the babies. "Dunno."

The wide grin threatened to split his cheeks. "But I can't wait to see the look on his face. We could sell tickets for that and make a ton of money."

Looking at the children a moment, he glanced at her. "Will they sleep for a while?"

Her look was guarded. "A couple of hours. They are very active and don't stay down long. Even at night I'll awaken and find them playing together. Why?"

"Where do you sleep?"

"I...?"

He smirked at her. "And you mentioned something about feeding me?"

Her expression settled into exasperation. "Well, you haven't changed."

"You'd be surprised how much I've changed." He pulled her up from the bed and hugged her. She was stiff for a moment before finally relaxing into the embrace.

"Fawn, I'm sorry you've had to face all this alone. I would have come back had I known. But I'm here now. We'll spend a couple of days getting things together, and then go find Sean."

She glanced up at him with a worried expression. "I've heard the land south of us is at war. So many tribes pushed together...."

He'd heard the rumors too but didn't know what else to do. "We'll work it out." He pulled her to him again as his expression hardened.

"I'm not unfamiliar with war."

———

THREE DAYS later Jim led their little caravan south. Before they left, he'd gone first thing to see Chouteau and presented the letter of credit given to him by Sean MacLeod. Using a small portion of that and his own money, he was able to outfit them for the trail with supplies and horses. It was a small matter and done every day for trappers moving through Kawsmouth and on north and west for the fur trade.

Turning to check on the two pack mules being led behind him, he smiled as Fawn rode up beside him holding their daughter straddled on the saddle blanket. The angry woman he'd first seen in the eating hall rode behind them with Sean's son held in front of her the same way.

He gave the other woman an uneasy glance. "Explain to me why we brought her along?"

She settled the squirming girl forcefully on the saddle before she answered. "It is the tradition of many tribes to let only the strongest warriors take a wife. This is true for the Nez Percé and keeps the tribe from being watered down by weaklings. Once that marriage is allowed, the warrior must also take the sisters of his bride into his tent."

He twisted in the saddle hard enough to strain his back. First to look at Fawn, and then at the other woman. The sister met his gaze with a stony expression.

"Oh, no. No, no, no. That is not going to happen."

Fawn's laughter was soft as she tickled the girl held in front of her. "You're a good man and strong warrior. This I know. You seem willing to make a life with me and your daughter. Is that not so?"

"Yes." He sighed, settling in the saddle and pulling the

slack from the lead rope pulling the mules. "Very willing. I thought of you a lot while I was gone. And the child kind of sealed the deal."

"And yet, here we are. Did you come back to find me?" Fawn tried to hide her smile behind her hand.

His answer was guarded as he nodded. "It was on my mind."

"Did you expect to find me?" Her voice was teasing.

Giving her a wary glance, he answered. "No."

"Did you expect to find a daughter that has your eyes? And regrettably, your nose?"

"It's not that bad." He looked at the girl closely. "And again, no."

"Did you expect to be riding to this Jones Mill with a woman and child, living as husband and wife? And followed by a woman holding the young son of Ghostrider?"

He snorted and looked at her. "That's an easy one. No. I did not."

"Then of all these things that you didn't expect, that are true and turned out for your good, and will keep you lazy and happy, how can you think she might not come to your tepee?"

He glanced at the sister's stony expression. The small smile forming as she watched him was almost scary. "I fear she'll kill me in my sleep. What's her name? She never speaks unless she's mad."

"You would never understand it. It has many different meanings."

"Fawn? What does her name mean? I have to call her something."

"It might be best not to call her at all." Fawn shrugged. "The closest in White man's language would be Angry Woman."

"Shit." He sighed and watched a couple of geese fly up from a small waterway. "Maybe I can sell her."

A low growl came from behind them.

"Well, it was just a thought."

---

THE NEXT DAY they rode along the banks of the Osage River when Jim asked Fawn something that bothered him.

"Fawn, why did you hook up with me? I know you didn't have to. Indian women have babies all the time and raise them. The fathers are rarely around, Indian or white."

She glanced at Angry Woman before answering. "Many reasons. It is a difference between the old ways and new ways. In the old ways, a woman's worth is in how much work she can do or how many children she can bear. Since laying with you and the fight within my family, I have lost my value in the old world. I speak Nez Percé, Arikara, Kansa, and understand many other people's language. I can do White man's numbers. Do you think this means anything to the Nez Percé warrior riding his Appaloosa war horse looking for a woman to conquer? No. He would throw me to the ground and have his way with me and beat me if I do not submit. It is their way."

He gave her a sideways glance. "All warriors can't be like that."

She hugged the little girl to her. "You think not? You should talk to Angry Woman. There is a reason she has that name."

"I'll take your word for it."

She paused a moment gathering her thoughts. "You give us much. You help and do your share. We have weapons to protect ourselves and our children. We have food to eat. When an Indian warrior falls, his family are the spoils of war. We have decided we will not be treated this way."

"You had a husband who treated you this way?"

She nodded, and then shrugged. Replying in a low voice, she said. "He liked to beat me because I would not always submit. Some women would have been happy with how many times he wanted me. But he as cruel."

"What happened? Did he fall in battle?"

Fawn glanced back at Angry Woman. "He was a strong warrior set in the old ways. In the eyes of our clan he could do no wrong. Everything he did to me was his right as a husband. Do you remember the high, chalk bluffs across from Chouteau's Post?"

He nodded. "It's at the bend of the river. The water is deep there, with a rocky shore. I've heard a legend that it's where young maidens with broken hearts leap to their death."

"And husbands who beat their wives." Cutting her glance at him, she gave a small smile. "Great warriors should not get drunk on white man's whiskey. Some say he stumbled. He may have been pushed. The only thing we know for sure is he could not fly."

"Sounds like a tragic ending." Jim laughed and was startled when he heard a giggle from Angry Woman. He grinned at her before his gaze settled on a spot where they could cross the river.

"Poor bastard."

# Chapter Nine

STANDING NEXT TO THUNDER, SEAN PEERED OVER THE saddle toward Ellen's cabin. A curtain moved but it could have been the wind. Likely was. Wishing wouldn't make her want him.

It didn't take him long to pack for the trail. He still had his oilskin, ground sheet and blankets rolled up behind the saddle. Leather bags hung on the front, stuffed full of food and supplies. Powder and ball were heavy and he questioned his decision to not use a pack animal. But after his experience with pack mules when he first came into this country, he'd never use them again. He vowed to do a lot of walking because Thunder carried too much weight.

Sighing, he walked the horse to Ellen's cabin. He couldn't think of it as his anymore. Before he could loop the reins around the hitching post, she came out and stood in the shade of the awning. After staring at him a moment, she held out a leather pouch.

"I know you don't like to go unshaved, so your razor

and soap are in the bag along with a few other items." She leaned against a porch post with her arms folded under her breasts. The hem of the shapeless housedress she'd changed into flapped in the breeze. Her hair was tied back with a black ribbon. Mourning?

Sean took the bag, a little amazed at how little he'd accumulated in a year, and looped the strings over the saddle. He tried to keep the bitterness from his voice, but like everything concerning her lately, he failed.

"That's all you have to say. Just, here's your stuff and hit the trail?"

"You're the one who decided to leave today." She stared at him a moment. "I don't suppose you'd come with me? I'm sure you could find something to do in the city."

Sean didn't know how his smile looked to her, but it felt sad on his face before it faded away. "You know better. I can't be something I'm not, no matter how hard you want it to happen. Whatever idea of me you have in your head, I probably never was nor will ever be. It's just not in me."

She looked wistful and smiled a little. "Oh, I don't know about that. I remember when you came here— bigger than life, ready to challenge anything and anybody. You stood up to every bad man you saw and either ran them off or killed them. For all your faults, you're a man. And I wouldn't change that for love nor money. How could a woman not fall in love with that? At least, a little bit." She paused and held his gaze.

"You're a strong man. But you're wild, Sean. I can't tame you and I don't know how I kept you this long. Times are changing, and I don't see you changing with them. You're like some of the far-traveling men we hear about. You're likely to take a notion and go away into the mountains and never come back."

Sadness seemed to be a painting covering his face in stiff oil. He could feel it—couldn't shake it off.

"Well, I think you're mistaken. Your wild man is looking to find some land north of here and settle down for good. Maybe open a trading post. This is becoming a settled land. It's a good opportunity."

He cleared his throat a couple of times before he could speak again. "My vision and hope was that you'd be by my side. It would be hard work at first, but I'm thinking a peaceful existence. I'm sorry you don't see it that way. I'd like to leave here believing you're not mad at me."

Her laugh was a hard bark that sounded painful. "Why should I be mad? You killed a man I admired and won't make any effort to live with me in Saint Louis. You're so anxious to get shut of me, you won't stay long enough to see me safely on my way—"

"—because I don't want you to leave. It's too dangerous...." His interruption startled her.

It's hard to argue with someone's back and that's all he saw as she disappeared inside. He wanted to make the argument that she wasn't making an effort to stay with him, but his mouth and brain were too slow. Maybe that was the problem. He was always too slow with her, or for her.

Thunder gave a surprised snort when he jerked the reins around and abruptly mounted. Sean gave the cabin one last look. The curtains hung limp and didn't move, defying the breeze, rigidly reflecting the anger held within. No sound came from inside.

His sigh was long and drawn out before he shook his head. "Well, hell."

He almost rode over Colonel Thompson when he wheeled Thunder around. Noting the colonel didn't look particularly angry and didn't have a squad of soldiers with him gave Sean hope. The encounter could go two ways—good or bad. He was curious enough to see.

"Sorry, Colonel. I didn't see you."

"That's all right." He gave a dismissive wave. "If you'd step down a minute, I'd like a word with you."

Sean walked his confused horse over to a hitching post and dismounted. "What can I do for you?"

The colonel took off his hat and rubbed his head. "Well, for starters, you killed one of my officers. That action is frowned upon in certain circles of military gentility."

A scuffing step alerted him that Ellen had come out on the porch. Well, why not? It concerned her too. "What about your circle, Colonel? You don't seem too upset at his death. How much trouble am I in?"

"With me? None at all. He was a foolish peacock of a man full of self-importance and flatulent wind. He also allowed the surveying party to leave without escort into hostile territory and once I learned the truth of it, I might have killed him myself." He turned and tipped his hat at Ellen. "No offense, ma'am."

She sighed and shook her head. "None taken."

He nodded to her as he continued. "Communication with Fort Smith is sketchy at best. I've written Ambrose into the post log as being killed in action. His relatives will get a medal in a year or so and a letter of condolence. They can make up stories of his prowess on the frontier."

Sean heard a gasp come from behind him but ignored her. "Then, what do you wish of me? He said you'd be leaving soon."

Colonel Thompson looked past Sean and addressed

Ellen. "Missus Mackey, we'll be having a short service for Ambrose. Given the circumstances, I thought to invite you. It will be in an hour. I understand if you'd rather not attend."

"As for you, Sean. I need your help. It's true, we are supposed to abandon the fort. However, my detachment will not leave until we catch those responsible for killing my family."

Ellen appeared beside them. "What killings?"

Sean briefly recounted what he'd found, including the bravery of the small boy. "If I ever have a son, I'd hope he does as well."

Her voice held a bitterness he'd never heard as she spaced the words out. "And he'd still be dead."

The colonel stared off into the distance, ignoring them a moment.

Sean continued. "Colonel, I made a promise to a brave young man. He was already gone at the time, but I think you understand. I'll not go back on that. I will find his killer. From what you say, I've already taken care of one of them."

He pinned Ellen with his gaze. "You have my promise to continue that search, even if it costs me a good woman."

Her gaze flashed in anger before she turned and went back inside. The only word he could think of was flounced. Was there nothing easy in this world?

He shook the soldier's hand, preparing to leave. "For what it is worth, my advice is to protect the fort. I'll be searching. When it's advisable, I'll send a message. You can mobilize then. There's no point in flailing about the forest with no direction."

The colonel nodded. "That makes sense. Thank you for that." He hesitated a moment, staring at Sean. "I don't suppose you'd take a commission? I seem to be short an officer."

Sean laughed, more from politeness than mirth. "No chance, but thanks." He glanced back at Ellen's cabin. "Although, she does seem to favor a man in uniform."

# Chapter Ten

MOVING DOWN THE HUNDRED YARDS TO THE RIVER, Sean then followed a well-traveled path leading upstream toward a massive spring. It was a relief to get out of the baking sun and into the shade of the forest. After an hour of travel, he smelled meat cooking and began to see tendrils of smoke following close to the cold water. The position of the sun and his grumbling stomach told him it was past time for a noon meal.

When traveling, meals were at dawn and dusk with some pemmican or dried deer meat in between. Domestic living turned him into a three-meal-a-day townsman. Absentmindedly rubbing his belly, he stopped a moment on the bluff above the spring and watched the activity below.

Water boiled out from the base of the bluff, turning into a racing, turbulent stream as it flowed away. He didn't know anyone, Indian or white, who knew how deep that water was or where it came from. That it came from deep in the earth was obvious—and it was cold down there. The pool was dark blue, nearly black at the deepest part, gradually fading to clear at the edges. From his vantage point he could see hundreds of fish poised in the water, all pointing upstream. He didn't know what food was carried in the water but judging from their size the fish must thrive on it.

A fire burned next to the water, shooting flames several feet into the air and was fed by several large logs leaning together. Naked children took turns running into the cold water to scare the fish. When the fish fled into the shallows they were speared or captured. The water was so cold the children would stay in the stream only long enough to splash around a few times, and then run to the fire to warm up. Judging by the amount of laughing and giggling, they loved every minute of it.

While a few men were trying to spear the fish, several women built drying racks inside a large hut with the sides missing. He figured the smoke was mostly to keep the flies from laying eggs in the meat.

The young children would bring a fish to one of the women. They would gut it, cut the head off and hang it over the fire by its tail. It seemed efficient, but looked like a lot of work for meat they were getting.

As he traversed down the hill toward the spring, a man stepped out from behind a boulder. Sean held up his hand in greeting, and then dismounted.

"Red Eagle. It's been a while."

"My friend." The Cherokee shook his hand white man fashion and then took off his hat and wiped his brow. His black felt hat looked like a pincushion for eagle feathers, and he slouched against the rock in a bright red shirt and homespuns held up by yellow gallus. As with most of the local Cherokee, he looked more like a settler than most of the men around Jones Mill.

"Did you come to eat or help catch fish?" The man

gave him a sly look and grinned. "Or, maybe to talk? I hear you got woman troubles."

He heard a hoot from the pretty woman tending a cook fire close to them as he answered. "Is there anyone who doesn't know my business? Have you sent a runner to the Osage yet? There's some Kickapoo west of here. Or the Delaware to the east? Maybe we should tell them?"

His friend shrugged, still smiling and not intimidated by Sean's bad mood. "Don't need to. They'll know by nightfall."

He gave Sean a sidelong glance and intoned in a deep voice. "When the Ghostrider talks, the echoes are heard in all the land."

Red Eagle easily dodged the rock that Sean threw at him.

He ground-reined Thunder in a patch of grass and walked to the fire, accepting a hunk of meat and fry bread on a bark platter from the woman and thanking her. She watched him closely for a moment. Now he knew how a prized bull on the auction block felt. With an abrupt move she turned, hiked her dress up and scrambled into the cold water to make a one-handed snatch of one of the smaller children struggling in the cold water. Depositing the little girl on a rock next to the big fire, she continued looking at him—shaking her head and mumbling to herself.

"Pay her no mind. This is Stands Tall." Red Eagle gestured toward the woman. "She's a medicine woman. Some claim she's Cherokee, but I think she's a Choctaw. Most of the Choctaw women are witches. She probably has an opinion on your problem. Matter of fact, she has an opinion on most things."

"So is this your wife?" He stopped eating a moment to stare at the woman. "She's beautiful."

The woman glanced over her shoulder at them as Red Eagle tried to explain. "Uh...no, she really is a medicine woman, and the men are more afraid of her than the Osage."

She glared at them a moment before she spoke in a clear, low voice. "Sometimes fear and lack of understanding are the same tree, just looked at from different directions."

Pinning her gaze on Sean, she continued. "I'm barren so that makes me unsuitable for marriage. I do my own hunting because no man will take me in. If I don't build my own lodge, I sleep in the forest with the animals."

"Uh, huh." He grinned and glanced at Red Eagle before he spoke to her. "If the men are afraid of you, how do you know you're barren?"

Sadness clouded her face before she pushed it away. "I had a husband and we tried for years. When there were no children he put me out of his lodge."

"Then he was no man." Sean smiled at her, enjoying the banter after the seriousness of Ellen. "You don't keep the young warriors warm at night? A good-looking woman like you? I'm surprised."

He watched her expression settle into hard lines. "I do not. I'm treated as if some disease has me in its clutches and it might rub off on them. And yet, they still eat food I prepare and let me help with their sick. It defies understanding."

"Maybe there are three sides to that tree. Wouldn't anger be more common than fear?"

She walked over and stood in front of Sean, holding his gaze with eyes that were so deep brown they seemed black as her long hair. Staring at him until he frowned and began to fidget, she finally spoke.

"You're the Ghostrider I've heard so much about. The way Red Eagle tells it, you killed most of the northern Blackfoot tribe all by yourself and made the rest run away like children. But he lies a lot. When I look at you all I see is a man." She walked around, looking him up and down. "Pleasing to the eyes, but still...just a man."

He often forgot the local Cherokee went to mission schools and spoke English better than most of the Whites settling in the area. He tried to get back to Red Eagle's comment.

"Well, I don't claim any of that but part of what you heard is right. Ellen is leaving as soon as new arrangements can be made. She wants to join her daughter in Saint Louis. We discussed it a bit, but conversation kind of dried up—so I left. Hell of a thing."

"Possibly you don't understand, until you walk around to her side of the tree." She smiled, and then it grew larger as she touched his arm. "Not to mention you killed her new man."

"Well, yeah...there is that." His smile matched hers. "To be fair, she didn't seem very upset about the loss. More peeved at me than anything."

"Of course. You are her man and you fought for her. She's proud of that, even if she pretends to disagree." She gave him a sideways glance. "But now, she has a problem. If she turns you away she has to leave. No one will try to lift her skirts for fear of being killed by the Ghostrider."

He shrugged. "I have little interest in her skirts. Not now."

The woman snorted and turned back to the fire. "So you say. Men always have an interest."

"What will you do. Will you leave?" Red Eagle watched them intently, gaze traveling back and forth between them. "The Whites are getting scared. Hell, I'm getting scared. There are too many hostiles around here. I fear bad things will happen soon if we are not careful."

Sean barely stifled a laugh at the wording. "Hostiles?"

"You damn betcha." He looked over at the woman. "Osage rode through here yesterday as we were setting up camp. Hawk was with them. Remember him? He looked meaner than a sack of snakes. That man is always mad about something. And I think he's grown. What is it with those Osage and how big they are? He looks like one of those giants in the white man's Bible. Anyway, he told us to leave or he'd kill all the men and children, and then sell the women as slaves."

"It's late summer. I thought he went north to hunt buffalo." Sean stared around a moment, finally noticing a few things he'd missed before. "Is that where most of your men are? Standing guard?"

Red Eagle nodded. "They'd rather do that than fish. I tried the fishing too. The water is so cold I haven't felt my legs since yesterday. My wife will be disappointed when I get home. Everything is frozen."

He paused at another hoot from the woman. "Besides, Hawk isn't one for idle talk."

"I expect your wife will thaw you out soon enough." Another thought sobered him. "So why are you here? Why not take your families and leave for safer grounds?"

"Where? When the Osage ceded land to the Whites, a great part of them moved west. But they still hate anyone not of their people. If you're not Osage, you are an enemy."

Stands Tall faced them again. "You're right when you

mentioned it's late in the summer. Our people need to put up food for the winter. We still don't have enough stored. And don't forget, we're not like some other tribes. We have homes and farms that need tended. We gave up tepee living a long time ago."

Red Eagle spoke louder, giving her a glance. "Hunting is poor. There are too many tribes here and the forest is hunted out. Our men come back from the hunt without deer, and the turkey they bring are scrawny this year...like there's something wrong with them. When you take the feathers off, they look like a buzzard. I am afraid it will be a bad winter. Even the fat red squirrels have left and the little Greys have taken over. There's not much meat on them."

"Usually we could kill a few bears," Red Eagle continued. "But the Whites are killing them to make bear oil to send south along with beaver skins."

Sean knew the practice of rendering the fat from the local black bear to make oil and grease was thinning the bear population, but hadn't realized how much.

"Don't lay that on our doorstep. Everyone is doing it, and you know it. When there's a market, people fill it—just like buffalo and beaver." He shook his head. "So, you're reduced to drying fish for the winter? No one ever got fat on fish."

Red Eagle nodded sagely. "But no one starves."

Standing and brushing his hands on his pants, Sean glanced at the river. It was time to go fishing. "Stands Tall, you don't have near enough women here. You need to send for more help."

Pulling a couple of the powder horn bombs from his saddlebag, he continued. "Red Eagle, why don't you position the men and children downstream in the shallows. If you have any kind of net, it would be good to use."

After giving him a long and strange look, Stands Tall grabbed a couple of young boys and sent them running into the forest. Red Eagle followed him to the bank of the pool. Everyone was curious, but did as he asked.

One thing he'd learned when clearing land by blowing stumps out of the ground. Black powder was fickle and it wasn't waterproof, but with a little timing?

"Bring me a burning stick from the fire."

He knew none of them had any idea what he was doing. Cutting the fuse to about six inches on the first horn, he lit it with the burning stick. He held it a moment watching the fuse, trying to estimate how fast it burned and then tossed it toward the middle of the pool —and got lucky.

Just as the powder horn hit the surface of the water it exploded. The blast was a loud clap of thunder that nearly deafened them. The explosion showered them with a fine mist and turned the clear water a murky brown, so he couldn't tell if he did any good right away. The first indication of success was a whoop from the men downstream and he turned to watch them scrambling to pick up the stunned fish floating on top of the water. Most were being tossed into a canoe.

Stands Tall came up behind them with a small smile. "That doesn't seem fair."

He glanced at her. "Do you want fair...or meat?"

The grinning men came pulling the canoe to the shore, laden with so many fish it was near sinking.

Red Eagle reached for the other powder horn Sean was holding. "Let me try."

"Whoa, now." Sean just laughed and held him off. "Maybe later. You've enough fish for now and I don't want to be calling you stumpy. If that goes off in your hand, you'll lose an arm."

The extra women arrived and the next hour was spent cleaning the fish and building more racks. He let Red Eagle throw the next one, but it hit the water too soon and the fuse went out. His next try was perfect.

While the Cherokee clan bustled about on the river-bank, Sean made camp under the trees and on higher ground. He hoped the breeze would stay in his favor and keep the stench away, not to mention the scavengers that would be coming in the night for the pile of entrails and fish heads.

He took Thunder down to drink again at the upstream part of the pool and then staked him out on a good patch of grass, close to the campfire. It wouldn't do for some enterprising warrior to try and steal the horse.

Not much of a fish eater, he took his bow and faded into the woods. Stands Tall said the forest was hunted out, but he knew any deer in the area would be coming to drink from the river and it didn't take him long to find a small doe. He dressed out the deer, gathered the haunches for himself, and then shouldered the rest. When he arrived at his camp, he deposited the carcass next to the drying hut. He knew the women would use everything but the skull.

Walking back to his fire, he cut a couple of sticks leaving notches at the top and suspended some of the deer meat to slow cook over the fire. The rest he wrapped in part of the deerskin and hung from a tree limb.

It was nearing dusk when Red Eagle joined him. He could tell the man was happy with the way the day went. "We must go back to our homes for the night. You're welcome to come with us."

Sean shrugged and shook his head. "No, I'll stay here. I'm not good company right now." He pointed to the meat hanging from the tree branch. "Take the meat for your family. I've more than I need."

Red Eagle thanked him and was wise enough to not argue the point. "All kidding aside my friend, we both know Ellen's a good woman. Whatever is working in her mind is keeping her from thinking straight."

His gaze lingered on Stands Tall. "Don't do anything tonight that you can't repair tomorrow." He patted Sean's shoulder and then rejoined his people, leaving Sean wondering what the man meant.

———

THE EVENING BREEZE turned cool as he watched the clan washing off in the cold water of the spring. Most of them stripped off their clothes and waded into the shallows to wash. He chided himself at his disappointment that Stands Tall didn't. She kept working, tending the fires of green wood that make the most smoke and laughing while the others washed and played, jumping around in the cold water. When the others left, she still worked.

The smooth, rock wall was a comfortable backrest as he enjoyed the cool evening. Looking around, he didn't see Stands Tall and was about to get up and look for her when he heard a quick step coming up the trail.

She stood close to the fire, wringing water from her long, black hair while framed by his small circle of light. She'd traded doeskin for gingham and the light blue cloth set off her dusky skin.

The coffee pot sat on a rock next to the fire and he gestured toward it, handing her an empty cup. "If you like coffee, it's hot and strong."

Liked it? She was into her second cup before she came slowed down. Casting around for a blanket to spread next to him to keep her dress clean, she sat beside him with a tired sigh, leaning her back against the rock. The fire crackled and flared for a moment sending sparks into the air, and then settled down. The heat felt good in the cool breeze coming off the cold-water spring. Shadows danced at the edge of the light and small animals growled and fought over the offal pile down by the river. It would have been a good opportunity to trap them if they wanted.

"You are troubled?" Her voice was soft as she turned to him.

He gave a surprised grunt, glancing at her. "It doesn't take much of a witch to figure that out."

She elbowed him in the side. "I have observed you many times, at the post and on the trail."

"You've followed me?"

Ignoring the interruption, she shook her head. "You act like nothing is wrong in front of people, but when you think no one is watching your gaze is far away. Your fingers caress the handle of your fighting knife, touching your blade the way you should touch your woman. What do you see, Ghostrider? What do you see when your mind reaches out beyond the trees? What is coming?"

"Nothing good." He scooted away slightly so he could turn and look at her. "What can I be, but troubled? Although bringing bad news for the colonel, I rode into the post a happy man. Content and happy to have found a better place to live. A place I don't have to constantly watch my back and where I can talk to friends. Then I killed a man I shouldn't have and lost a woman I'd counted on. I can't imagine why I'd be troubled."

Stands Tall filled her cup again and poked at the meat with her knife point before sitting down. "I think you are looking from the wrong side of the tree I talked about.

You are like most men, only seeing what's in front of you. Let me tell you how I see it. A man challenged you for your woman in front of people that respect you. That is nothing new in this world and you handled it as a man should. You may not have realized it at the time but from what I hear, he asked for what he got. As for your woman?" Her shrug was eloquent as the spoken word. "Who knows? I don't think you've lost her. She handled things badly, but that's no sin. We make many mistakes going through life. All of us. Even you."

She chuckled. "Especially you. The White man's saying of a bull in a china closet fits you perfectly. Sometimes these problems can be fixed...sometimes not. This time?" She shrugged again. "Who knows."

He frowned at her, wanting her to understand. "It's not just the physical—what happens between a man and woman. She said nothing like that happened and I believe her. But something did happen to give him the idea she would leave with him. Whatever she did, or how she acted around him, put me in a secondary place in her mind. That should not be. At that point, she'd already left me."

Her gaze bored into his eyes a moment. "Sometimes the ability to reason makes you do it too much."

"You mean I'm thinking too much?" His interruption was rewarded by another elbow.

"You are a good man and speak well, but you need to re-think what you just said. Again, look at the other side of the tree. A woman's mind cannot be reasoned by most men. It has been said we are a breed apart, just compatible enough with men to have children. Any two people can look at the same thing and see something different. That happens most of the time."

She reached forward and drew a figure in the dirt.

"Think of the White man's numbers. I can draw a six in the dirt, but standing on the other side it looks like a nine."

"Looks more like a 'b' to me." He grunted as her elbow caught him in the ribs. He gave her a hard look. "Sitting next to you is getting to be painful."

Moments later he picked up the thread of conversation again. He didn't like the way his voice came out—even as he spoke, he thought of a petulant child. "We have nothing left but reason, if she won't talk to me. I can only make decisions on what I see."

"Then make the effort. Walk around the tree. See something else."

Settling back against the rock again, he watched as she got up and began slicing meat from the haunch hanging over the fire. Fat dripped into the small blaze making it flare and sizzle. He began talking and told her all of it.

His mind wandered back to the killing of his wife and son, and the retribution against the Blackfoot. Weary of fighting, he'd come south only to step into a new battle. Ellen's daughter was captive to a French slaver, allied with renegade Osage.

In a strange turn of events, his nemesis Buffalo Shield became his friend and saved his life. With that fight over, he and Ellen had spent a lot of time together—until today. In his mind, the worst part was the betrayal. She should have talked to him about her problems, not someone else.

Up to now it had been a peaceful time for him. He had a home and a woman to share it with. Life was good. But then the dreams started again—dreams that left him standing in the middle of the night searching for the enemy, hands grasping his fighting knife and sweating like he'd done battle. Now, he was afraid to sleep.

She clutched his arm and gave it a shake. "Look at me. When you talk or think of your past, you go away somewhere. Come back to me, Ghostrider. Stay with me. On this earth...on this ground."

He took the meat offered to him and tried to listen to her, but the day was catching up with him. He yawned so hard his jaw popped.

Her soft voice calmed him. "I fear you fill the heart of this White woman so much she bursts with pain, but she does not truly understand what you are...who you are. She thinks she does. Her needs are immediate and in front of her. That is all she sees. I fear she will act on that."

"What do you mean?" He paused with meat in one hand and coffee cup in the other.

"Your problem is you keep trying to be something you are not. That gives her hope as she tries to make you into something she thinks is safe for both of you. No matter what you think, you are a warrior not a shopkeeper. Your woman may understand that, but it is deep within her—she can't bring it to the surface because she is afraid. A woman wants a peaceful home and life. Sometimes we don't realize it takes a warrior to make that happen."

He yawned again. The warm fire and full belly was getting to him. "Well, even warriors need to rest."

She ignored his try at humor. "You need someone by your side who understands. You are not the civilized man your white friends think you are. I think you are more savage than even your Cherokee brothers think. Even the Osage step lightly around you. I have seen this."

He tried to fight past the tiredness of his mind. Her

soft, mesmerizing voice relaxed him more than he could remember ever being. "What are you offering?"

"That's the man in you talking. I don't offer what you think...at least, not now. Perhaps in the future? I cannot lay with you, unless you and your woman have an ending and I don't think that will happen. But you need a guide, someone to talk to. A friend."

"I have friends."

She gave her classic hoot. "Not that many. And I'm beginning to think you need a keeper. I cannot fight your battles, Ghostrider. But maybe...just maybe...I can point you toward the right ones."

He tried to suppress it, but finally gave up and yawned again. "Sorry. I'm worn out. You're welcome to share the fire, but I'm about done in." He barely registered a blanket being thrown over him as he fell asleep, still leaning against the rock and gazing into the fire. It'd been a long, emotional day.

And the dreams came. The world was on fire and he fought—fought hard against the crazed enemy, screaming and dancing through burning buildings. But through it all a soft voice crooned to him, and he felt a cool hand caressing his head, wiping sweat from his brow—and he slept again, deep and undisturbed.

He woke when a wren started fussing in the nearby bushes. The morning light was gray with no hope of sunshine in the shadowed forest. His head was in her lap with her fingers entwined in his hair. She slept soundly, her breathing so slight he wondered if his dreams had sucked the life from her. As he stirred, she woke and smiled at him.

"You've come back to me. I was afraid you would not. You fought a mighty battle last night."

Sean abruptly sat upright. "I'm sorry you saw that."

"Saw it?" She stood, rubbing her arms and stretching her back. "I have bruises to remind me that I was there in your dreams. But don't trouble yourself. I have a better sense of who you are and a good idea why Ellen is afraid and confused. Do not worry. Something always happens to make the bad things of yesterday seem small."

"You mean like something worse?"

Her gaze was pensive. "Sometimes, sometimes not."

# Chapter Eleven

STONEFACE WATCHED THE SETTLER'S CABIN FROM THE trees bordering the shadowed valley. He hoped to strike before the sun peeked over the hills and burned away the mist. Although not needed, fog would give cover for his men to get close. It was already hot and muggy, something his warriors had yet to grow accustomed to—most were used to the weather of the north along the Canada border.

His scouts told him there were three men and two women in the dwelling. And no dogs? Every Indian village and wise settler had dogs for sentinels—and a steady source for meat in lean times.

Smoke rose from the chimney, only to collect around the cabin and drift toward the ground in the still air, adding another layer of low visibility. The smell of frying meat and coffee made his stomach rumble. He smiled. Perhaps they'd cooked enough for all?

A man came out, gave a wheezing cough, spit into the grass next to the porch, and then walked to the small stable. With a mild curse or two, and the rattling of a bucket, he began milking their cow. Head trapped between manger posts, the animal was restless and troublesome.

Another man came out of the cabin, hitching suspenders over his thin shoulders and pitched hay to the horses in the corral, first filling the trough in front of the cow to settle it down. Nothing looked amiss, just another day in their frontier paradise. Had their dreams been met? They didn't appear to have the awareness of hunters. Would they next try and tear up the earth to plant their crops like the women of the Osage?

The warrior pondered waiting longer, although the fog might lift and they'd lose their cover. Milk was an acquired taste, but he liked it with fried meat and bread. With two women tending the fires he was sure there'd be plenty to eat. Perhaps he'd keep them alive long enough to feed his men? After all, they had no plans to kill them. Not right away.

A third man came to stand on the porch holding a rifle. It amazed Stoneface how the Whites could live with no thought for safety. This man should have come out first as a guard to check for any danger to his home—not that it would have made any difference. The warriors were well hidden and well versed.

The appearance of the third man ended the waiting. The men were all accounted for and it made them easy prey. The thought of the coming strike was like White man's whiskey, quickening his blood and his breathing. He could imagine the pleas. Questions would be shouted by the victims. How could this be happening to them? What had they done wrong? And the biggest question? Why? They would beg for mercy and it would fall on deaf ears because there were no answers to those questions. At least, none that would make any sense to them. And their God would not help them, no matter how much they called and pleaded for intercession. He never had.

Stoneface raised his battle axe and pointed toward the man with the rifle. The near instant flight of arrows buzzed in the air and the man fell writhing in the doorway. Frantic screaming came from inside as the women tried to pull the wounded man into the house. As he watched, the clearing filled with his warriors rushing with muted footfalls to their tasks. There was no war cry or shouting, just a silent methodical attack. All his men knew their tasks.

The settler milking the cow set the bucket down carefully and then tried to run. Did he think he'd be back for it? Stoneface shook his head. There was no battle. The white men offered little resistance. More important, it was over without a shot from the rifle being fired, preserving the silence of the forest. Screams wouldn't carry far, but gunshots would. It bothered him that they had yet to find an enemy to test them. His men were getting soft and complacent.

Stoneface rose and walked into the clearing to join his men. As he moved to the door of the cabin, he paid close attention to the arrows that struck the man in the doorway. Only one was a kill shot. He would find that bowman and use him more, although sometimes wounding was desirable.

He stopped before entering the cabin, gazing around the clearing. Catching Big Hand's attention, he held up four fingers and then made a circling motion. Guards would be set. Disappointed guards, but they knew better than to disobey.

Big hand trotted over to him. "What of these two men?"

Stoneface regarded them a moment. "They call to

their God to save them. Strap them to posts with their arms outstretched and leave them. If their Jesus hasn't saved them by the time we're through with their women, then kill them."

"Why do you hate Christians so?"

He gazed at his second-in-command a moment. "Black Hoof, brother to Tecumseh and a great prophet has told us this. It does not matter if they are of The People or White. They are nothing but witches who bring disease to our people, luring them with presents and whiskey, making them give up the old ways—ways that have served us well for many lifetimes. I have seen this. They drive us from our lands. Their priests take our children away to be schooled in the white way...not Shawnee."

"Do you punish those who believe in this God, or just those who teach its ways?"

Stoneface looked at his lieutenant. "All. Wherever I find them. There is no difference."

At a woman's shriek from inside the cabin, he knew his men were not waiting. While being the best fighters he could find, his followers also had a voracious appetite for women—a problem that might be their downfall if not controlled. But for now...? Warriors remaining outside turned and moved toward the cabin, talking quietly among themselves—much like he'd seen Whites do for their funeral processions. The men tied to the posts cried and begged to be let go. Neither asked for the women to be spared. Tears streaked their dirty faces as they strained against their bonds.

Were there no men among the Whites? A Shawnee would never stand and beg for his life. The white women fought harder than their men. Stoneface spit toward them and turned to enter the cabin.

He had no doubt the captives would be there when he returned.

————

AN HOUR later Stoneface stood on the veranda of the cabin, sated and relaxed. A quiet, civilized breakfast and the good mood of his warriors gave him a feeling of euphoria. Watching his men use the captives for target practice was amusing. Of course, the men were long dead.

The cow had been killed and butchered. They'd wrap the meat in hide and carry it to their next campsite before cooking it. There was no point in tempting fate by staying, although it was a good place.

Big Hand came to stand with him. "The sentries have been replaced and we've picked a trail. We can leave anytime."

"Then let's leave this place. When we go, stay behind a while to see if anyone shows up. It might lead us to more settlers."

At a sharp whistle from Big Hand, the men assembled in the clearing. Stoneface raised his hatchet and pointed toward the forest. "We go."

# Chapter Twelve

SEAN STOOD BY A DYING FIRE, COFFEE CUP IN HAND. A cold updraft came from the spring and he shivered. It was time to leave his camp by the river. Ellen was the most important thing on his mind...in his life. He needed to go back and talk to her but couldn't think of the right words. Avoiding the conversation wasn't helping, but every thought of her was clouded with anger. Maybe it was too soon to talk, but he didn't know if the time would ever be right. Or, if he'd ever find the right words. Common, everyday words may not be enough.

Stands Tall had returned to tending the fires and drying fish. He watched her a minute. From a distance she looked like any other person tending to her chores. Up close, her mystic nature came out. He reasoned that was why the Cherokee men called her a witch. Of course, anything they didn't understand had to be witchery. That was true of any race of people. Sometimes he followed that line of thinking himself when he thought of females in general. He hadn't found one yet that he truly understood.

Lost in thought, it took a moment before registering the rapid footfalls approaching. Thunder's ears were pointed up the hill behind Sean's camp, so he turned that way. His hand gripped the fighting knife at his side, only to relax when Red Eagle came sliding down the embankment.

He poured a cup of coffee for the man and waited for him to catch his breath.

Finally... "I was at Jones Mill this morning when a report came in about a settler family being killed. The soldiers are getting ready to go there." He gave Sean a long look. "I thought you might want to get there first. The soldiers will erase any sign with their clumsiness."

Sean thought a moment. If there were a threat to the settlement and the outlying families, they needed to find out quickly. It was late in the summer for any kind of uprising from the locals, although it couldn't be ruled out. The killing of the surveying party was on his mind. Added to the Shawnee who attacked him? Things were happening.

"Whose place? How far?"

"A family named McGill. I don't think they've been here long." He settled his felt hat, stooping to pick up a feather that dislodged. "I remember your friend Shay trying to convince them to settle closer to the fort but this place was an abandoned homestead—ready-made, so they moved right in. It's one, maybe two hours from here. I figure we could beat the soldiers if we hurry."

Sean thought a moment and then nodded. "All right. I'll break camp. I expect we can get there faster on foot. Can you guide me?"

He'd noticed Stands Tall coming up to them. Putting two fingers in her mouth she made a piercing whistle. Thunder jumped and snorted while both men put hands over their ears. She grinned at them while two boys came running from the riverbank.

"These two will clean up the camp and take Thunder back to the fort. We should hurry."

Sean shook his head, giving her a wary glance. "Now wait a minute. You're not coming with us."

She tied one end of a long piece of rawhide around her waist, looped the extra between her legs, pulled it up and tied it to the string already looped around her. The action pulled up the middle of her dress tail and it looked as if she were wearing baggy pants.

"I made a promise to you." When he didn't respond, she continued. "Did you think a woman's promise made in the dark wouldn't survive the light of day? Is that the way your word would be? We're wasting time."

His gaze was still on her dress. "Well, that's a handy trick."

Sean sighed, ignoring Red Eagle's grin, and then picked up his bow and quiver. "All right. Let's get going."

Stopping next to Thunder, she pointed to his rifle. "Are you taking this?"

"Not this time. It's heavy for running and the one shot is a disadvantage telling everyone where you are. I expect there'll be plenty of those when the soldiers arrive."

Alternating between running and walking, it took little more than an hour to thread their way between the hills to the homestead. It lay in a wooded valley next to a small stream feeding into the White River.

Paused on a slight rise in the trail, Sean stopped and took a deep breath. Stands Tall was close behind him and he could feel her panting on his shoulder. Red Eagle stood to the side to get a better view. No sound came from the clearing below and a crow cawing in the distance made the silence stand out.

Sean listened to the crow a moment. It didn't sound quite right, and then it stopped. He knew one thing for certain. Crows were gregarious creatures and once started, would fuss and call to each other all day. The birds were probably wondering who was trying to imitate them. They were not alone with that thought.

While his companions muttered to each other in a mixture of English and Cherokee about what they saw below, Sean kept his gaze on the surrounding forest. Just because things looked peaceful, discounting the bodies tied to the posts of a corral, didn't mean they weren't being watched. From the distance he could see red streaks of blood on the limp, hanging bodies. There was no need to hurry.

He pulled an arrow from his quiver. "Don't let down your guard. I'm sure whoever did this is long gone, but they might leave someone behind to watch...actually, I'm sure they have. You two can wait here and be on your guard. I'm going to look around a bit. We need to insure this isn't a trap set for us or the soldiers."

"We'll go with you." Her voice was firm and Red Eagle glanced at Sean and shrugged.

His idea was to circle the place and find any trail or sign. He'd seen dead bodies before and felt no need to rush down to the cabin. The Army patrol would be there soon enough. Once they started moving, it was slow going, stopping often to listen and using any cover they could find. There was nothing unusual and the crows still weren't talking. A few minutes later, on the far side of the small valley from where they started, he kneeled next to the stream. They'd found no sign up to this point.

Someone had fallen and left a scuff mark on the slick

limestone next to the water. A large handprint shown in the mud where the man got up. Sean put his hand in the print and it was larger than his. And he was a big man. He looked around a few minutes before standing and gazing into the forest. It was hard to tell where they went but he felt the war party was long gone. Since there was no defined trail of several men leaving, they must have scattered and would likely meet up somewhere else.

They approached the clearing, somber as a funeral march. Re-affirming that the two men tied to the posts were dead, Sean and Red Eagle cut them down. Stands Tall went on toward the house. As they finished, he heard a soft cry from the home and watched as she came out on the porch. Tears coursed down her cheeks to be wiped away with the back of her hand. Her mouth opened a couple of times but no sound came from her. She finally pointed inside. Glancing at her he realized she was crying in anger, not anguish.

He faced the door with more dread than he could remember. "Do I really need to see this?"

She hesitated a moment and then her nod was a quick jerk.

Shoulders slumped, he turned to his friend. "Red Eagle, if you would keep watch for us, I'd appreciate it. Let me know when the soldiers come."

"Good. I can't think of anything I need to see in that house." The man nodded, watching them for a curious moment before moving away from the house toward the edge of the forest.

The dirt floor muffled his dragging feet as Sean walked inside. Stands Tall's presence behind him was reassuring. A man lay along a wall, just inside the door. He'd been wounded with arrows, one still broken off where someone tried to pull it out. It looked as if a toma-hawk did the rest of the damage.

His impression was that it was a quick raid, breaking into the house before defenses could be set. The front door was intact but the main room was a shambles. If this were a war party, some things didn't add up. Clothes were scattered everywhere, so it would be hard to tell if any were missing. The men outside were stripped and their clothes lay tossed about. Usually any useful clothes were taken to wear or for trade. Pots hung above a fire-place and most raiders would have taken those—knives lay on a bench in plain sight. Why weren't those taken?

No matter how vicious the raiding party, most would have women at home tending the fires. Brass pots and iron skillets were prime plunder, hardly ever left behind.

The answer was apparent. Raiders will kill you for what you have, be it money or goods—sometimes women. But this? He would guess it was not personal. Gazing around he nodded. This was a message, crude but effective.

News of this, coupled with the murder of the surveying party, would place terror in the hearts of the settlers. Maybe that was it. Scare people into running, either away or to the post. Which led to more questions. Why? He doubted this band of raiders had enough men to attack the post with any hope of success. Too many unanswered questions bouncing around in his head gave him a headache.

Sean glanced at a table next to the fireplace. In a room with nothing left unbroken or not methodically destroyed, a plate sat on a table and was placed in front of a chair. A half-eaten chicken carcass lay on the plate—a pewter mug sat next to a bucket that once held milk. He ran his finger around the rim. Fresh milk. Someone sat and had a meal while all the carnage was taking place? The view was serene, almost normal. Added to the whole, this added a different layer of crazy to the cold-blooded cruelty he'd seen.

Stands Tall leaned her head against his shoulder a moment and then pointed to another room. Moving through a splintered door hanging on a leather-strap hinge, he stopped abruptly. Two women sprawled on the bed. Broken dolls tossed away when their use was at end. Blood soaked the blankets beneath them and splattered the walls.

He was in danger of adding his breakfast to the mess until he felt her hand on his arm. Was she giving strength, or drawing it? For the moment it was shared. It was apparent the women tried to barricade themselves inside the room. All the pieces of furniture were by the door, only to be pushed aside when the room was broken into.

After a sharp intake of breath her voice hardened. "Who would do this? None of the tribes we know would do this."

He glanced at her. "It's been my experience there's no limit to cruelty in man—Indian or white. And it's the second time I've seen this in just a few days."

Her glance was tearful, astonished. "Their breasts?"

"The same." He shook his head, staring out the door. "We got a real special kind of sick animal running around somewhere."

She paused, looking perplexed as she gazed around the cabin. "I find it odd. We found three men and two women. One bed."

He waited her out, watching her walk around the main room, turning over clothes with her foot and looking at the shelves—curious of what she would come up with.

"I would expect to find children here, with two women available." Her voice was soft. "But there is no sign of them."

He shrugged. "Some don't want children. As for the rest? None of our business. The world is a funny place, full of isolated stories and circumstance. We all have our sins to worry about. Maybe they were hot bunking like some big city hotels do."

Her eyebrows raised as she shook her head, wary of his answer. "What is this...hot bunking?"

"In larger cities, especially where there are mines or factories, people work in shifts. Some at night, some during the day. The men working at night sleep during the day, use the bed while the other is at work. Then they trade off. The bunk is always hot."

"I don't think I like these cities you speak of."

She was still shaking her head when Red Eagle called from outside. "Soldiers come."

The woman pulled on his arm. "Help me. Others should not see them like this. Please."

He agreed. There was little enough dignity in death, they'd give them what respect they could. They found blankets and rolled the women into them. As they finished, Colonel Thompson walked through the front door of the cabin.

"Are there more bodies in here?" His voice was brusque, clipped with anger.

"There are." Sean put the flat of his hand against the man to prevent his entry. "Colonel, one dead body looks much like another. Let's go outside. You've some decisions to make."

The man sighed, seemed to resist a moment and then

turned away. Once outside he spoke to Sean. "Do you have any idea who is doing this?"

"None at all."

They watched a few soldiers come out of the small barn carrying a pick and shovel. "Do you think the people responsible for killing the surveying party did this?"

He nodded with a grim expression painting his face. "I'd bet on it. The treatment of the women are the same, and very...unique. Before getting back to the post, I was attacked by two Shawnee. The next morning I found the surveying party. My guess is it's a raiding party of maybe twenty men. A small enough force to move quickly and remain hidden—large enough to do a lot of damage. They'll do their deed, then split up and meet somewhere later to plan the next attack. And it's possible they have someone watching to see our reaction. A sure bet, I'd think."

"Damned Indians—"

"Not true," Sean cut him off. "Colonel, you need to understand something. Most of these damned Indians, as you call them, are just like us. Hell, they all are. Their ways are different, hard to understand sometimes, but they just want to be left alone to raise their families in peace. There are some that hate us and want us dead or gone. You'll find hotheads on both sides. I think whoever is leading these attacks won't stop until he's dead, or moves on to easier prey."

"For what purpose?" The colonel gazed around the clearing. "Even animals don't kill with no purpose."

"I'm thinking the purpose is to make people mad and afraid. When that happens, people do stupid things." Sean shrugged. "That's my opinion."

———

THE SOLDIERS FINISHED with their burial duties and started to group around their horses, not a few watching Stands Tall. She strode over to Sean, dress tail still tied up for running.

Glancing at the soldiers, she rolled her eyes. "Those men would do better watching the forest."

"Some things are better to look at than mossy old trees." Looking around, Sean asked quietly. "Where's Red Eagle?"

"He left to warn his people and try to get his wife to go to the safety of the settlement."

Sean nodded, watching a couple of magpies chasing a crow across the treetops. "Think she'll go?"

"She's very stubborn. I doubt she'll leave her home."

He turned to the soldier. "There's your answer, Colonel. My suggestion is to get back and defend the fort. This is the third incident of attacks. We can't ignore it. Send runners to the outlying farms and warn the people. I'd use some of the Cherokee hanging around for this. It'll get done a lot faster. Try to get settlers to come in for a few days. I'm thinking we'll know soon enough what's going on. I feel there is purpose to all this. We just don't know it yet."

The soldier didn't like being ordered around. "Maybe we should scout around, see if we can find them. I have some good men with me."

Stands Tall snorted and Sean shot her a warning glance before turning back to the colonel. "Our agreement was that I'd try and find out what's going on. I'll hold you to that, if you don't mind. Otherwise, you're on your own to do as you wish."

Colonel Thompson bristled. "Do I have to remind you of my authority?"

"It's not a matter of authority. You're starting to sound a bit like Ambrose. You say your men are good soldiers. That may be, but they're not good out here. Look at them. They're through with the burial detail and standing around smoking and talking—not a care in the world. No one is facing the forest. I don't see any sentries. Saw a man go to the edge of the forest for a call of nature...didn't take his weapon. There's not a woodsman among them. If that raiding party came back, you'd lose most of your men before they fired a shot in defense."

Sean shrugged. "This isn't a contest. It's a matter of using your assets to the best advantage. Your advantage is the fort. Don't let yourself be drawn out."

"Perhaps you're right." The colonel looked at him a moment. "All right. We'll return to the settlement." He gazed around the forest. "You be careful."

"That we will, Colonel. That we will."

# Chapter Thirteen

YOUNG BETH MACKEY STOOD ON THE BANK OF THE Pomme De Terre, a free-flowing tributary of the Osage River, which in turn would take them to the Missouri River and on to Saint Louis. She stared at the men below as they bustled about loading stores on the flatboat that would take them on their journey.

A trapper tried to hobble his packhorses on the front deck. The boat was rocking side-to-side and as she watched, one horse went pitching over the side. The men on the boat cursed and then laughed when a couple of trappers stumbled into the water trying to retrieve the lead rope of the horse.

She was glad the trapper hadn't completed his job. The horse would have drowned with the hobbles on and she couldn't believe the rest of the horses were tied that way. She'd been told there was rough water ahead. The melee below changed her opinion of them. First she thought they were just inept. Now, she figured the men were dumb as a bag of rocks.

With a small smile, she glanced toward the trees and

where Buffalo Shield talked to a couple of strange looking Indians. She didn't like them. While her adopted grandfather was clad head to toe in buckskin, the strangers were naked except for their loincloth knife belt. They had shaved heads like the Osage, but didn't have their look. These men were different and looked dangerous. And arrogant. She'd been taught by Sean MacLeod that the difference between a mountain lion and a tabby cat, and how dangerous they were, was not so much in the size of their claws but in their attitude...their willingness to use them.

That realization swept her smile away. A quick step brought her close to her horse and her bow, a shorter version of Sean's English longbow. He'd crafted it just for her before she left and made her practice with it every day. She'd always thought she was strong until trying to pull and release arrows at fifteen per minute, and hit her mark. But he'd made her do it, while Buffalo Shield looked on with a smile. She'd practiced every day but the Sabbath.

Stringing the bow in one swift, practiced motion Beth watched her adopted grandfather shake his head and step back as one of the men spoke sharply to him. When Buffalo Shield put his hand on the knife at his waist, she pulled the bowstring and released it with a loud thrum, just to let them know she was there and that he was not alone. Sean had told her stories of ancient warriors who, before a battle, would bend their bows and sword blades and release them all at once—the thrumming echoing a thousand strong as their war cry.

Buffalo Shield turned and gave her a sharp look that she returned with a smile while inspecting the iron-tipped arrow in her hand. The strange looking men stared at her a moment. One spit on the ground before the two men turned and disappeared into the forest. Her frown matched her grandfather's as he approached her.

"Who were those men?" Her gaze still tracked the spot they'd disappeared into the forest, making sure they didn't come back. Her first impression was that she didn't trust them.

"They were Shawnee." His voice was a deep rumble. "Their land is far to the north, between the land of the Blackfoot and Lakes of The Fathers."

"Why so far from home?" Watching him she could tell he was troubled.

He shrugged. "They're gathering warriors but wouldn't tell me the purpose." Gazing at the forest where the men had disappeared, he continued. "They have much anger and hatred, wanting to know if I followed the white man's God."

"Which one?" She glanced at him. "Every preacher that comes through seems to have a different one, and only they can interpret the meaning."

"You are saying the words of Ghostrider. I don't think he is a good teacher about that." Buffalo Shield shrugged and offered a wry smile. "Though he may be right."

Beth didn't like any of the situation. She did not feel safe and knew Buffalo Shield felt the same. They'd traveled north from Jones Mill with a group of traders for two weeks to arrive at this place. Some of the party went on north toward Kawsmouth, the junction of the Missouri and Kaw rivers, while others stayed. Although they moved with the group of men during the day for protection, Buffalo Shield would not camp with them. He and Beth would always pull away at sunset to find their own place. She believed they could have made the trip in a week if they weren't encumbered with the trappers.

Turning toward the river, she shook her head at the circus unfolding below them. She'd decided and a small smile of relief graced her face as she gave him a mischievous glance.

"I can't seem to move my feet, Grandfather."

Buffalo Shield looked at her feet. "I don't understand, Little One. We are on dry ground. Are your bones so old you cannot move?"

She snorted, knowing he was onto her already. One of her favorite pastimes was irritating the old warrior. Smoothing down the front of her shirt, she glanced at him. "Little One? I'm not so little anymore. Look at me. I'm twelve summers and about as tall as you, which makes me taller than most men we see. They are starting to look at me."

He gave her an amused look. "I sharpen my spear every night, my blade yearns for their blood."

Her hand clutched his arm. "Don't worry. Any boy who seeks me must first see my grandfather." She paused a moment. "Or Sean."

"Not your mother?" His tone was curious as he watched her.

She paused a moment, giving the question some thought. "No. She'd never be able to decide. Look at what she's doing with Sean. She is afraid to stay in this country but does not want to leave him, so she makes them both miserable. My mother is caught in a trap of her own making and doesn't know how to get out. Sometimes I think she's addled."

"You are wise beyond your years."

"But back to this." She continued, waving toward the river. "I have made a decision. I cannot do this."

"*You* have made a decision? All by yourself?" His voice mocked her. In his world, young girls did not make decisions. Even if they were abnormally large for their age, strong and smart.

"You know I never wanted to come in the first place." She thought for a moment, glancing at his puzzled face. "After we've journeyed to this point, I'm unable to move forward. I cannot. My home is behind us. It's where I belong."

She pointed over her shoulder. "Besides, if that boat settles any more it's going to be taking on water. I think it will sink regardless of all they can do. Even if it doesn't, I do not want to spend weeks rubbing shoulders with that lot down there. I doubt you do."

The long-drawn-out sigh from the old Blackfoot medicine man brought a smile to her face. She patted his arm. "This is wrong, Grandfather. I think we both know it. We've faced danger before. I can't leave our people—we're going home."

His gaze sharpened as he watched her. "And who are your people?"

"My mother is white. My father Osage. I feel no more allegiance to one than the other. My heart is drawn to my brothers and sisters—the Osage and Cherokee." Her glance caught his eyes. "And perhaps the Blackfoot?"

He didn't appear surprised at her decision. The old medicine man replied in a mild tone as he leaned on a spear adorned with feathers—she knew the scalps were taken off in deference to her. "Your mother will be angry. You agreed to leave for your safety. Going back will not make her happy."

"She is already unhappy." Beth snorted and shook her head. "I did not agree with the move and was forced to leave. This St. Louis they want me to live in? Do you think I would be safe there? Surrounded by men like those below? How will we hunt, how will we live?"

"I know nothing of this Saint Louis." He shrugged, watching the men below. "But we cannot live off the land forever. There are too many people. Even now it is getting hard to find game."

Beth shook her head. "Well, if it is to be that way, if that is what is to come, the time is not here and not now. I want to go home and that home is in the forest and hills behind us." She gave him her best little girl look. "Please?"

He frowned. "Stop it. You turn an old man into a mindless child, ready to do your will. But you speak to my heart with much wisdom. We'll do as you wish."

Buffalo Shield turned and faced the forest. "You must understand there is much danger in going back. Those Shawnee have nothing but anger in them. They are looking for warriors to join them and I fear they might be headed toward the fort."

She stood in thought a moment. "Maybe that's why Sean's spirit dreams are coming again. If an attack is coming, all the more reason we must go back. If for no other reason but to warn them."

He shook his head, glancing at her. "Perhaps that's the very reason we should not go. It is not safe."

"I understand, Grandfather. You want what is best for me." She leaned against him a moment. "But this is a danger we understand and must face."

———

THEY MADE GOOD TIME, pushing their horses hard and then leading them so they could rest. The large party they'd traveled with before, while offering protection, progressed at a crawl and only held them back. A camp was made before sundown. When darkness approached they put out the fire and drew back into the trees for safety.

Beth stared up at the stars through the canopy of trees. "What am I, Grandfather?"

She knew he was awake, watching and listening to the night.

His voice was a soft rumble. "A barking squirrel. A magpie disturbing my rest."

"I wonder about my place. In which world will I live? I'm torn between my father's Osage blood and my mother's people."

She heard his sigh and then the silence stretched out to the point she thought he wouldn't answer.

"You must take the best from both. Don't choose either but make your own path. These things will become clear when you are grown."

"Really? Grown? I'm ready now. Many Indian maids are married at my age, or are soon to be."

"And die in childbirth because they are too young. I have seen it. Sometimes the mind matures before the body and takes you where you're not prepared to go. Don't be in such a hurry."

She felt around under her groundsheet for an offending rock. "I'm strong for my age."

Another sigh...long drawn out. If a sound could show disapproval, this one did. "Your strength worries me. Ghostrider trains you like a warrior. Sometimes I wonder why he does this. Your mother should be the one teaching you how to be a woman and the duties of a wife."

Beth snorted. "I'm not sure she knows how." Finding the rock, she tossed it away. "Maybe that's the blood warring within me. I should try and be both."

"You have time. Just remember, you cannot be what all people want."

"I hope you are right." She sighed. "Good night, Grandfather."

"Finally." Grunting, he stirred around searching for a comfortable position for his old bones.

She lay in her blankets, staring through the canopy of oak leaves at the stars. Her pillow was another blanket rolled against her saddle. The horses pulling grass was a soft, reassuring sound along with crickets and tree frogs. An owl hooted, causing her to smile. Some believed it was an ill omen, signaling death. And it did, for small animals—mice and rabbits. The night teemed with life as they all went about their business. And all were sentinels. If they stopped...? Sighing, she closed her eyes but sleep was slow in coming.

———

HOURS LATER, when the predawn darkness shrouded over them, the crickets and tree frogs stopped their music. Beth's eyes popped open and she sat up in her blankets. Her mouth parted slightly and she searched the darkness with every sense she had. In the dim light, she saw a doe and fawn moving away from them. They'd never come this close unless spooked. Something was moving through the forest, making no sound but an occasional swish of limbs being pushed aside.

She picked up a pebble and tossed it at Buffalo Shield's sleeping form. His breathing changed and became quiet. He was listening too. There was no doubt it was a party of men. Other than one shade of darkness moving within another, their movement could only be tracked by the lack of forest sounds—quiet where the men passed and picking up again after they left.

When they were almost gone, one dark form stopped and seemed to be listening. Eyes strained wide, Beth struggled to see anything in the darkness as she held her breath. She caught a faint whiff of their campfire and wondered if the man smelled it too. After a few moments, the man moved away. Quiet as she could, she let her breath out, trying to still her thumping heart. From this point on she promised she'd be ready for an attack in the dark. At least, the best she could be. And make damned sure their fire was out—the coals dead.

Finally, when she was sure the party was gone, she moved to Buffalo Shield and spoke softly, stretching up to his ear. "Should we follow? Moving in darkness like this, we know they are up to no good."

She could picture him shaking his head as he whispered. "We should not. That was a war party. For them to move so quickly through the forest they will have scouted the trail beforehand. So they know the land and we do not. We'll wait and see what daylight brings."

They pulled their blankets farther back into the bushes and sat, waiting for the dawn. Buffalo Shield was a few feet from her, leaning against a tree as she spoke again. "Do you think...?"

A rock bounced off her shoulder. She shut up.

# Chapter Fourteen

BETH STOOD STARING INTO THE FOREST. IT WAS TWO
mornings after listening to the war party move past in
the darkness and Buffalo Shield had gone out before
dawn to hunt. They were short on rations and still a few
days travel from Jones Mill.

She glanced at the sun filtering through the canopy of
leaves. He should have been back an hour ago. Unable to
picture him having an accident or hurting himself, it was
just as unlikely that he'd miss getting a deer. Something
was wrong.

Knowing he would want her to wait, she paced a
moment, hands on hips and listening to the forest.

After another hour, all waiting was at an end and she
wasn't going to sit around any longer. He could be hurt.
Breaking camp was a simple matter of gathering bedrolls
and lashing them to the back of her horse.

After thinking the passing war party might have
smelled a rekindled fire, they'd built a different one by
digging a hole in the ground and building the fire in the
bottom. It wouldn't support a large blaze, but they didn't

need one. As she was leaving, all she had to do was kick the dirt over and fill the hole, burying the coals and all evidence of their passing. It was simple enough and she wondered why they hadn't always done it that way.

Since he'd left in the dark, there was little effort in concealing his trail and she could follow easy enough. He would ride away from the camp until he saw a deer trail, or any sign they'd passed—often a rubbed place on small saplings. Even if the rub was old, it didn't matter. Deer were creatures of habit and always used the same trail unless disturbed by hunters—man or beast.

Minutes later she reined in her horse, a cold knot forming in her belly. More hoof prints joined his trail, planted over the top of his. He was being followed. And if he could be followed...so could she.

Like she'd been taught, she moved to the side of the trail and sat motionless a moment looking at the surrounding forest and listening. How close were they? Did Buffalo Shield know he was being followed? If he'd been ambushed, she'd heard no shots. Of course, that didn't mean much. Most frontiersmen and Indians were loath to use their rifles. They were noisy and limited the shooter to one shot before reloading, maybe three shots a minute if lucky. Bad things could happen while reloading.

She couldn't wait forever. A soft voice and squeezing knees urged her horse forward. Wary of ambush, she scanned the forest around her. She followed the trail, stopping often, not wanting to miss any sign. She could turn away and run—should run, it was the wise choice. But he might need help and she couldn't abandon him anymore than he would abandon her.

It was an hour of slow traveling before boisterous laughter and shouting carried to her from a clearing ahead. Maybe he was with friends and maybe, just maybe, he was all right. With a quick prayer she slowly, silently, pushed forward.

———

BETH PAUSED in the dappled sunlight under a canopy of oak and maple, clutching her stomach against the knot of pain trying to escape. For a moment it was a battle between being sick or soiling herself—but she knew this was nature's way of giving her an excuse to flee. She took a deep, calming breath and focused on the problem before her, resisting the urge to rush forward.

A dozen paces into the clearing Buffalo Shield lay across a rotted log, arms outstretched, bent over backward and staring at the sky. She stared intently at him, couldn't leave without knowing for sure, hoping, praying for some movement, some sign he was alive. Nothing moved. No eyelids fluttered. No fingers twitched. His chest did not rise and fall.

His wrists were nailed to the log with arrows. A shadow crossed the clearing drawing her attention upward as the silhouette of a bird rose in the wind. Maybe an eagle taking his spirit away? If he were alive, he would give her assurance that this was a warrior's end, better than old age and being dependent on others. He would rather go out cursing at his enemies, fighting until he was overwhelmed.

If given a chance to argue, she would disagree. Still a vibrant man, he'd gathered age and put it in his pouch to be used another day. To her, he'd been ageless. She'd rather have him here, on this earth, no matter how old. Listening to his wisdom every day would be better, but it was not to be. That choice was not given to either of them.

Glancing at her back trail, she gasped. In the distance, she could see her fate loping toward the clearing, heads down looking at the trail she'd left. Three men, naked but for loin cloths and moccasins and scant minutes away. She knew the men of the forest and their skills. She might escape...maybe. But then, there was her grandfather. He'd told her once there was no point in running from an angry bear—you'd just be tired when it killed you.

With a brassy taste in her mouth, she nodded, mouth set in a grim line. Something cold and hard rose within her. So be it. If this was her day to die, it was a good day.

She slow-walked her horse toward the body. The hoof-falls were silent on the soft ground. It would be hard for her enemies to pick her out against the backdrop of the forest behind her. And they were too busy celebrating to look.

Buffalo Shield was pinned to the log with arrows and she knew he'd been left to die. Even if the men coming up behind her didn't find her right away, the celebrating warriors would come back for unbroken arrows and find her tracks. Once that happened, the chase would be on and it was a race she would lose. There were too many of them and no safe haven she could run to before they captured her. The trappers and traders back at the river would be long gone, if not drowned. There was no safety there. No safety, in any direction.

A long sigh escaped, turning into a sob—caught, and stifled with resolve. Dismounting, she dipped her finger in her grandfather's blood and made a cross on his forehead. Didn't know why. She did not feel Christian on this day. She could pray for him but wanted the Christian God to ignore what she was about to do. Or as she'd heard her mother say...seriously mangle a commandment.

She plucked an Eagle feather from his hair and stuck in her own.

If there were time, she would sit with him and remember all their journeys together. If there were time, she would talk to his spirit about how much he would be missed and all the things they could have done. If there were time, she would cry. If...there were time. But not today. Maybe in the afterlife if tears were allowed. Depending on which God took her soul.

She put her hand on his shoulder, talking in a whisper barely heard beyond her own lips. "I'm sorry, Grandfather. Sorry you didn't make it to the land of your fathers'. But your family is waiting for you. You will find them. I know you worried about old age. Now your aching bones are at rest. No more pain. We don't know what the afterlife brings, or how swiftly you go. Wait for me if you can. I am coming."

Something happened to her, like she was doused with water and it washed away something old, revealing someone new. Sadness came with it. There'd be no time to explore this new person. The cold anger and stillness within her was a blessing.

With a steady hand and final clutch on his shoulder, she stood. Only then did she raise her gaze to the men beyond. She shuddered and ground her teeth fighting the fear that flushed hot and coursed through her body—fear that threatened to turn her guts to water.

But she would not run. She. Would. Not.

She recognized the Indians who looked different and had argued with Buffalo Shield at the river. Her adopted grandfather would tell her to run—get away. But where? These men would hunt her down like wolves after a deer. Miles from home, she had no desire to leave this spot in the forest where the tall fern and towering oak gave peaceful shade. It was a fitting place for her ending. Glancing upward through the canopy of leaves she could see the eagle circling. The spirit of Buffalo Shield waited for her with open arms. This was her day.

She now understood what Grandfather had told her about himself and Sean MacLeod—the Ghostrider. He'd spoken to her of the cold and bitter rage that still possessed the man's soul. The same man who'd taken the time to teach a young girl to fight. It was odd, in a way. Buffalo Shield was a great warrior and taught her how to hunt in the forest and care for herself, but he deferred to her adopted father. The respect was deep between them.

Ghostrider taught her how to fight. And now she understood. She would not grow old, nor hold a baby to her breast. This day she would die. But not alone. Her mouth settled in a grim line. Not. Alone. Her thirst for revenge would be slaked by the blood of her enemies. There would be a reckoning on this day.

The men were loud around their fire as she stepped to the side of her horse, already judging distance and trajectory. Steady hands were belied by a trembling chin. Tears overwhelmed her eyes for a moment as she leaned her head against the side of the horse. And the horse knew, skin rippling but making no sound.

Sadness overwhelmed her before resolve firmed her lips and a toss of her head sent the tears away. Her bow and iron-tipped arrows were rolled in a bundle and tied to the side of the saddle by a single rawhide string. With a deep breath, she pulled it and released her weapons.

Ghostrider had told her of faraway ancestors and how they fought—she would do the same. As she strode to stand beside her slain loved one and stuck her arrows into the moss-covered earth, she visualized those same spirits that haunted Ghostrider's dreams and kept him awake at night—blood-streaked men with blue war paint, running through fire, screaming their defiance at those who would enslave them.

*Come to me! Are you only good to haunt a man's soul? Are you cowards? Are you afraid of a new battle? Come to me! Consume me with your fire. It will be a remembered battle to feed the spirit world. I need your strength!*

A musty odor rose from the moss-covered floor of the forest—released by the points of her arrows jammed into the soft earth. The bow was made especially for her in the tradition of Welsh bowmen. No Yew could be found so it was made of boxwood and was extremely hard to pull. But she'd been taught to bend the bow by leaning into it, not by pulling the string by strength of arm.

Retrieving the string from its waterproof pouch, she was thankful they'd found a way to keep it dry. A wet string would stretch, making the bow useless. Threading the bottom notch with the string made of silk and hemp, she pulled down the top notch and latched the other end of the string over it. Her movements were sure after long hours of practice. She took pride in the fact that some men couldn't pull the string of her bow back to their ear.

Gazing at the throng of warriors, she pulled the string to her chin to test its tightness and then let go, giving voice to the sound that had quickened the hearts of many an Englishman. The thrum of the bowstring was like a covey of quail flushed from hiding beneath your feet, echoing between the trees. It gave them warning, but it was tradition—and she would die by tradition this day. She would inflict revenge on those who killed her grandfather and by doing this, give tribute to the ancestors of Ghostrider. It would be enough.

Even in celebration, the warrior's ears were tuned to the forest around them. The thrum of the bowstring caught some of the men's attention but they couldn't find the source right away, many gazing in different directions —listening, eyes searching. Always fearing ambush and attack, they searched the foreground first, looking for immediate danger. The hesitation would cost them.

Raised on stories of men who seemed larger than life and then having two examples of her own in Buffalo Shield and Sean MacLeod, she felt resolve. Most girls her age didn't think of death, but being raised on the frontier and captured by slavers last year gave it substance to her. She did not want to die. She did not. There was a Cherokee boy...her head shook, chiding herself.

Running away was useless. They'd find her. If she was to die, she'd make her family proud. The survivors of this battle would sing her song for generations. She knew her lessons and had practiced often. Both her mentors were amazed at the strength of her arms. Taking a wide stance for balance, her arrows were close to hand when she reached down. Just like practice. Fifteen pulls to the minute. Find your mark, pull and release. The mantra played through her mind as men scattered before the onslaught of her arrows while others stood in amazement, as if she were some magical nymph come from the forest.

Mark. Pull. Release. The thrumming was hypnotic to her ears as she hardly noticed the strain in her arms. She'd had thirty arrows at her feet and when she glanced down was surprised they were gone. Looking up, she dropped the bow next to the body of Buffalo Shield. Pulling her knife, she knew Ghostrider would be proud. Sad but proud.

She wished she had his fighting knife, though her arms were tired and holding it would be difficult. The field before her was littered with the bodies of her enemies—thrashing in pain or dead. She tried to swallow but couldn't summon enough moisture to do it. Buffalo Shield was avenged. Her glance moved upward to see the eagle still circled...waiting.

Be patient...I'm coming.

Brush rustled behind her and she whirled. A warrior stared at her, his face a mask of hatred with glittering eyes caught in the sun. As he continued to look at her, she gave him a cold smile. Raising her knife, she sliced the blade across the deerskin and into her chest. With her free hand, she took the blood and spread it on her face. She held her blade cutting edge up, eager to plunge into the soft parts of his body.

The man held his palm up to halt those moving behind her. His hand held a pipe-axe adorned with hair and pouches of skin. She flinched when she realized what the blood-streaked pouches were.

Turning, the man sunk the blade into a tree. Staring at her, he drew his knife and cut himself across his bare chest, mimicking her as he spread the blood on his face. Matching her smile, he strode toward her.

She wished for water with her body still running on adrenaline but thrust the feeling away. In a few moments her thirst would be gone and she took small comfort in that. Palms dry on the handle of her knife, she moved to meet him. They were a few feet apart when she spoke in French, which most Indians understood at least a small amount because of dealing with trappers. He must have understood because he stopped with a startled expression.

She was surprised her voice was strong and clear. "The man at my feet was a Blackfoot warrior and my grandfather. Buffalo Shield's spirit will be proud of me this day as he rests in the arms of his loved ones on the spirit trail."

Her voice hardened as she pointed her knife at him. "But your days are numbered. The Ghostrider will avenge my death as he swept through the Bloods of the Blackfoot Nation to avenge the loss of his wife and child. None were spared. I will be avenged! He will come for you."

She nodded at him. "You will kill me today, but your death song is already singing on the wind in the trees—your dying breath moves the grass at our feet. When Ghostrider comes, do not beg for your life. He will not show mercy."

"All of you." She glanced to the side as more men surrounded her. "You are all dead."

The man in front of her spoke. "Who is this Ghostrider?"

She took a deep, calming breath and stood erect and proud, knife at her side—longbow at her feet. "He is my father."

Blinding pain startled her, dropping her to her knees. As darkness took over, she knew a rule had been broken, drummed into her by Ghostrider. Never talk when you should be fighting.

# Chapter Fifteen

Stoneface watched the girl lying on the ground. Knocked senseless, she still dug her feet into the soft earth trying to move.

He looked at the man next to him, who'd walked to them from the campfire. "How many?"

The man shrugged, pulling his knife. "Eight are dead. Many more are wounded and may die. Twenty if you count them." He leaned over to begin cutting off her clothing when Stoneface put a hand on his shoulder.

"Bind her, and keep her alive. She is not to be harmed."

She groaned, digging in her feet again as Stoneface looked across the clearing at the carnage wrought by one person—a girl. If only his men could do as well, and had her spirit. He shook his head at the thought of it.

He nudged her with his toe. As a woman, she would never give birth to a girl. She was too strong. Nothing but boys would come from her. And with the right husband? Someone who could make her submit?

Stoneface looked at those gathered around him. "We

will find this Ghostrider she spoke of and kill him. When the girl sees her father killed by my hand, she will submit to me. Her anger will be broken."

The warrior turned his hot gaze toward Stoneface. "She spilled our blood. We must kill her now!"

He stared at the man until the warrior looked away. "For what? Revenge? How do you avenge all the lives taken by such a young girl? The dead warrior's spirits will hide, never to cross over to see the Great Spirit. If anyone finds out about this, your shame will make you take your own life—if I don't do it for you. No one must hear of this."

As the warrior walked away, Big Hand came to stand beside him. "We have lost too many men. This will never stay a secret, much as we want it to. Shall I kill him? He is weak and will never stop talking until he dies."

Stoneface watched the retreating warrior a moment. "No. We are short of men now and need every warrior, at least for a time. Use him, and others like him, to lead us into battle. They will fall first."

He pointed to the girl. "Guard her. We can use her to draw out this Ghostrider. There is a fort ahead of us and he must be there hiding behind its walls."

Big Hand gazed into the forest. "This Ghostrider may not be so easy to kill if he is her father. Think of that. If he trained her..."

"It will not matter." Nudging her with his foot again, he drew a groan from her. "And be careful with this one. She's no longer a child and not yet a woman. That's a middle ground that knows no fear. She is dangerous... more so than most of our men."

Big Hand's voice was soft. "I know we weren't here to see her attack. Surely the men must have been surprised or fooled in some way. She was lucky."

"Oh, they were surprised." Watching his men drag bodies from the clearing, Stoneface replied in a low voice. "I saw no fear in her when she faced me. She was eager. Most of her arrows found their target and the men were moving, trying to hide. I don't think luck had anything to do with it."

One of his men walked up and handed him an arrow. "See the points on the shaft?"

Stoneface flinched when he ran his thumb across the iron-tipped point and cut himself. "Bring all her arrows to me. If they are broken, bring the heads. I've never seen anything this sharp."

"Where will we find them?"

Big Hand shoved the man and made him back away. "Fool. You will find them stuck in the men. Dig them out. She did not miss."

Stoneface looked at his second-in-command. "What news do you have for me?"

"Things are going as planned. We found a Cherokee family living by themselves." He handed over a bag of trophies. "The men are satisfied for now."

He gave Stoneface a troubled look. "It seems their thirst grows each day. Their thoughts are not of spreading fear through the countryside. All they want to know is where to find the next woman."

Stoneface shrugged. "Both means achieve the end. We must clear the land for ourselves. When we attack the outlying homes, it will either drive the people away, or into their fort. Either way we shall kill them. Our journey to this place called Oklahoma has little appeal for me. We shall stay here."

"There are many tribes living here, with greater numbers than we were told. They are being pushed from the east much as we're being pushed from the north. What of them?"

He nodded to his lieutenant and shrugged. "I have thought of this. The Osage have gone north hunting buffalo. They will return in small groups and be dealt with. The Cherokee and Delaware will go to this land called Oklahoma. Some have left already. Any of the tribes that are moving will not be harmed. The time is right to take over."

"And the men? They won't sit long before going hunting."

"Tell the men there will be plenty of women after we take the fort. They need to keep their minds on the task before us. We will have all this land after we finish. Once we have the fort, they may go, or stay, as they wish."

Standing by the body of Buffalo Shield, Big Hand noticed Beth's bow. Picking it up, he pulled on the string until it was halfway to his ear. With a grunt, he tried again with no better luck.

Bow in hand, he looked at the unconscious girl. "How is this possible? She must be stronger than some men."

Stoneface gave what passed for a smile with him. "Stronger than you? There are many things to be learned from her. How does she pull her bow?" He shook his head. "I'm more interested in where she got the arrows."

He looked at the camp and the wounded men. Kneeling, he drew a crude, wavy line on the soft forest floor, and then made a circle on one side. "This is the river to the west and the fort on the other side."

Using the handle of his pipe axe, he drew a half-circle leaving the fort in the center. "Send the men into this area at first light. They must kill or run off anyone living there. When we attack the fort, there must not be anyone at our back."

"And the wounded?"

Stoneface glanced at the men gathered around their fire. "Give them tonight. If they cannot be on the trail tomorrow...kill them."

When Big Hand didn't reply, he clapped the man on the shoulder. "Come, set the sentries. You will camp here tonight. Keep watch. She will be like the coyote, a trickster. Do not be fooled. I will take some men and scout the fort. Once we learn their habits, we can walk in and take it."

"Is it wise to keep her alive? We cannot guard her all the time."

"It is wise because I wish it." His gaze bored into Big Hand. "Do not fail me."

Big Hand hesitated a moment before speaking. "I have other news of this Ghostrider. Word has come that the man called Ambrose has been killed. There will be no gold. Perhaps we should bypass this fort. An ill wind blows here."

Stoneface glared at his lieutenant a moment. "We would have killed him anyway, so it makes no difference. His gold was never needed. Now, go to your duties."

———

BETH AWOKE PROPPED against a large boulder, idly wondering why she was drooling on the front of her shirt. Staring at her bound ankles, it took a moment for her mind to come out of its fog. Her head snapped up and she winced at the sharp pain in the back of her head. Mindful of her head, she took a slow look around, making as little movement as possible.

She was on the other side of the clearing from the warriors. Judging by their position, Buffalo Shield's body would be about fifty paces behind her. Her feet and hands were tied with rawhide cord that cut into her wrists. She was supposed to be dead. Glancing wildly around the clearing, the words she used to curse herself weren't what she'd want her mother to hear.

She was supposed to be dead—needed to be dead—not captured. Now she was a prisoner of the animals who'd killed Buffalo Shield. Remembering the ornaments tied to the pipe axe held by the ugly warrior she'd talked with, her stomach went cold and she fought nausea.

A shout from the campfire drew her attention as one of the warriors held a shank of hair high above his head and pranced around. Turning her head away, she imagined it belonged to her slain grandfather. The movement made her stomach roil and heave as she leaned to the side to gag and wretch her meager breakfast. Which made her head hurt more and cause even more sickness.

A piece of cloth landed on her bound hands as a bowl of water was placed by her. "Clean yourself."

It was in English, but the voice was enough. He'd been sitting by the rock all this time. It was awkward with her hands tied in front of her, but she soaked the cloth and cleaned her face. Rinsing it out, she took the cloth and tried to reach the back of her head. It was too hard and she gave up.

"Lean forward."

Reluctantly, she did as he asked. Were there ways she could escape? She'd been captured by slavers the year before but they had no interest in killing her. These men were different...deadly. She looked to the sides trying to see a way out. She'd made her peace with death and expected it. Her plans were not to live to fight another day, nor to be a captive and warrior's plaything. Running would mean death, but perhaps a better death than this one. And she vowed to herself to not sell her life cheap.

"Stop moving." Rough hands moved her hair aside and probed the back of her head. "No blood. You have a hard head."

She squirmed to a better sitting position. A chance would be coming. She had to get free. "You were supposed to kill me. Why didn't you kill me? Who are you? Why am I here?"

"So many questions." He walked around so they could face each other. "I want to kill you; it would give me much pleasure."

He pointed to the men prancing around the fire. "They want to kill you. Well...after they make a woman of you."

Glancing at the warriors, she expected fear to weaken her knees, but found nothing but anger to stiffen them. Her chin lifted as she stared at the man in front of her. "It's what I expect from such as you."

The man stared at her a moment before tapping his chest. "I am Big Hand." He held out his hands showing the right was much larger than the left. "You are being held because Stoneface has taken a liking to you. He has visions of using you as a brood mare to raise his sons. He thinks, with your blood, his sons would be mighty warriors."

"I'll die first."

He laughed. "I have no doubt you will wish you were dead. He sees you as someone great in spirit."

The wet cloth felt good to her face. "And you don't?"

"You?" He spit at her feet. "All I see is a dirty little girl who should be skinned alive."

"This dirty little girl killed your warriors." She

noticed some of the men at the fire looking at them. One raised the flap of his breechcloth and waved it at her.

"A trick. The men were surprised somehow, but they won't talk of it. Someday, if you live, you must show me your tricks."

Her gaze met his, and they stared a moment. She watched him flinch as she gave him a cold smile. "Given a chance I'll show you a few...I promise. But for now, I need to rest. My head hurts." She picked at her buck-skins, running a finger through cuts and tears. "I could use something to repair my clothes."

She leaned back against the rock as she heard him walk away. Closing her eyes, she suddenly clenched them hard to stop tears from leaking out. She was play-acting as two people. One was hard and didn't care if she lived or died. But there was a scared little girl hiding inside that she couldn't let out. Not now. Maybe never. One thing was certain. She would not submit.

Her grandfather must have seen deep into her soul. He'd once told her she had two hungry wolves inside of her. One was kind and gentle. The other vicious and evil. How she turned out in life would depend on which she fed the most. For now, she would feed the evil one. She needed that strength.

Beth lurched awake when a pile of clothing fell by her side. Big Hand walked away and she glanced at the pile of garments. When she realized where they must have come from, bile rose in her throat. Moving her bound hands through the pile she saw blood spots on several garments. Starting to push the bundle aside, she felt something hard.

A large knife in a sheath was hidden in the clothes. An accident? Not likely. Gazing at the man walking away, she knew Big Hand would like nothing better than for her to try and escape. Then he'd have an excuse to kill her. Or maybe he thought she'd kill herself. Partially pulling the blade from its sheath, she tested the edge. It was sharp, with a long, wooden handle. Possibly a skinning knife stolen from someone's kitchen. Resolve hardened her gaze as she stared at the warriors. They'd found whiskey and were stumbling drunk. Her chance would come and she'd give Big Hand what he wanted. But not what he expected.

It was the same as before. She could run, but would be caught. What they did not know? She had no intention of not getting caught.

The sun was behind her, hiding her in the shadow of the rock. It also showed that no one was standing close behind, their shadow would show. She could see Big Hand standing at the fire, listening to the warriors shouting and screaming as they built themselves into a rage. In silence, using the bundle of clothing to hide her actions, she cut her rawhide bonds.

When the shadows were long, they came. As she watched, Big Hand tried to intervene, halfheartedly, she thought, but was shoved aside. Five warriors strutted and stumbled toward her. The one standing in front of her was naked except for breech cloth and moccasins—and blood streaked in dirt and filth. His head was shaved, leaving a scalp lock hanging in the back.

Spittle hit her face as he yelled at her with a broken speech of French and English. Some words were foreign to her but she could guess the meaning. "Witch. What manner of trickery did you use to kill my friends? You cannot be allowed to live."

He took a step toward her, lifting his breechcloth and grasping his genitals, shaking them at her. "You will know what we do with women before you burn. Even little girls."

With a feral scream, she leaped to her feet, stumbling a moment from lack of circulation. The warriors stood in surprise, one covered his mouth and bleated like a startled calf. Cutting edge up, Beth stooped low with the knife, almost like she was laying it on the ground and then with all her strength brought it up, slicing the warrior from crotch to breastbone. He screamed as he stumbled backward, trying to hold everything together.

The warriors broke and ran, screaming about a *Mishipeshu* and Night Panther. When she looked to the side, Big Hand was grinning at her. Shaking the bloody knife at him, her voice was rough and loud with anger. "That's one trick. Find me and I'll show you another."

Running into the forest, she made a quick circle of the small clearing. While the men were all yelling drunken threats at each other and pointing toward where she'd disappeared, she walked to their fire and found her bow. They wouldn't be as good, but she took a quiver of arrows. With luck, she'd be able to give them all back before she died. She held no illusions of escape.

———

THE MOON WAS full and bright, casting shadows in the forest when Big Hand watched Stoneface and ten of his warriors return to the clearing. Their first sight was the bloody corpse stretched out by the rock. Moving to where the fast-sobering men huddled around the fire, he gestured for Big Hand to join him.

"Who made a woman of Running Dog?"

"That *Wazhazhe* girl you captured."

One man spoke, sitting on a log next to the fire. "She

is *Mishipeshu*, the panther hiding inside the body of a trickster. She should have been killed when we had a chance."

Stoneface gazed around the darkened clearing before bringing his puzzled gaze back to the warriors. "How did this happen?"

Big Hand shrugged and spat toward the men around the fire. "These men found whiskey and were crazy, wanting revenge. When I tried to stop them, I was pushed aside as they went for the girl. They wanted to burn her as a witch, after they used her. Somehow she had a knife and had cut her bonds. When Running Dog stood in front of her, bragging about what they were going to do, she cut him open."

Stoneface snorted. "He was always bragging of what he hid in his breechcloth. Of more importance is where did the men get whiskey and where did she get a knife?"

"These things I do not know."

"You do not know." Hands on hips, Stoneface didn't speak for a moment as he stared at Big Hand. "What I see is my men getting drunk and a small girl killing a grown man, and then escaping into the forest while you watched. These are mysteries with no answers."

"We were surprised."

"You are my right hand, second-in-command of our warriors. And you failed. If it happens again, I'll gut you myself. I may do it anyway. Do you understand?"

Big Hand stood straight. "I do."

Stoneface nodded. "Kill these four drunken fools as a lesson to the others. They were told not to bring the white man's whiskey into camp."

The ten men who came with Stoneface quickly dispatched the drunks and then dragged them into the forest by their heels.

"Big Hand, you will take five of these men and find the girl." He paused a moment. "When you find her, kill her and bring my trophies as proof."

"It shall be done."

Big Hand tried to keep the smile from his face as they gathered weapons, water bag and trail mix. Stoneface had lost sight of their goal, giving the girl his attention when it should have been elsewhere. There was no way they could have kept her around, with her lording it over the warriors as some kind of princess. Supplying the whiskey had been easy, the knife easier. He was surprised she'd used it so well, and shook it defiantly at him, but that just helped the plan. Now, all he had to do was finish the girl and things would be back to normal.

A wind came up, bringing clouds that hid the moon. It was a bad omen. The rustling of limbs and leaves would make it hard to find her if she was running. Deer would be restless, bounding through the trees and spooked at the slightest noise. It would be a distraction, but he could not wait. He motioned to the men and led them into the forest.

# Chapter Sixteen

BETH STOOD IN THE DARKNESS LISTENING TO THE
Shawnee warriors try and explain their fear. All people
are superstitious to some degree, Indians a little more
than most. She could feel that from both sides of her
lineage. Her white mother would scoff at their fear and
then toss salt over her shoulder. Her Osage father? She
had no idea. But all the Indians she knew had their own
set of superstitions.

It was hard not to run when the four drunken
warriors were killed. Somehow it didn't shock her. But
she stood...waiting. She must feed the *Wahya* soon. The
peace-loving wolf on her left shoulder was shocked at the
brutality. The evil wolf on her right was restless, wanting
more blood.

And now she had a name. For whatever small time
she had left, it was fitting. *Mishipeshu*—Night Panther.
She liked it. And she would do all she could to live up to
the name.

When Big Hand led the five Shawnee warriors

through the other side of the clearing, the side she'd run from, she watched and listened. When they were gone, she stared hard at Stoneface. He sat, ignoring his five remaining men, looking into the fire—something Ghostrider had told her never to do. When you glance away from the fire, all you see is the reflection—like looking into the sun.

What could the evil within Stoneface possibly be thinking about? What was his *Wahya* telling him? Was he feeding it? Or was it feeding on him?

It was time to go. Big Hand and his men came first. Stoneface would wait. But should he? Unbidden, her hands notched an arrow. She could try and kill him now —cut off the head of the snake. But freedom called to her. If she missed, she'd have two groups chasing her. She'd set her mind to dying a warrior's death, avenging her grandfather. Better to get away and set an ambush that she alone controlled. While Ghostrider had taught her to fight, Grandfather had taught her the ways of the trail. They expected her to leave in head-long flight and panic. She would not.

Beth felt a small rock under her moccasin. Knowing she was invisible in the darkness, and could disappear in moments, she picked it up. It was a long throw, but she was strong. The rock sailed through the air and bounced once before hitting the fire. Embers scattered and the remaining warriors jumped, gripping weapons and chanting. If only she could mimic an owl. The times she'd tried her grandfather had laughed. But it would certainly spook the warriors. The owl hoot was a portent of death.

Stoneface stood looking at the enshrouding, dark forest. He may as well have been looking directly at her when he smiled. She shivered and turned away. She'd try for Big Hand. If she couldn't ambush him some way, she'd try and go home to alert Jones Mill. Her mother would be shocked. Ghostrider would smile.

For the first time, she thought of living.

———

THE DARKNESS in the forest was complete. Big Hand stopped his men after a slow-paced advance through the brush and trees. His men bumped into him when he stopped. It would have been funny on a different day. If he knew the trails and land, he had no problem with fighting at night. But he did not know this country and was wise enough to realize someone living in the area would have a huge advantage.

His voice was a whisper. "We will camp here. No one can be found in this darkness. We sound like children, stomping around trying to scare up a rabbit. Lay by the trail. No fire, no talking." He could tell they were not taking this seriously.

He stood a moment, waiting for his men to settle down, fixing their position in his mind. As he turned to step off the trail, something whipped by his head and skipped off a tree, and then rattled into another. He dropped and scurried into the darkness. She'd tried to kill him. How? He'd made no sound. No moonlight filtered through the canopy of leaves above. He was not backlit by anything.

Holding silent, he gripped his knife. He didn't think she'd come close. But then, he thought she'd run away and not attack. When she pointed her knife at him and promised more tricks, he'd put the threat down to the bravado of a child. He had to change his thinking. She was no child at all. Maybe the men were right. They'd captured a *Mishipeshu*, a Night Panther. Now they were paying for it.

There was an old tale. A man climbed into a tree and reached into a squirrel's nest, becoming instantly impaled with teeth and claws. Drawing his hand out, he called for help. When his fellow hunters advised him to throw it down and they'd kill it, he replied that he could not. The squirrel wouldn't let him.

It may be the same for the *Mishipeshu*. She may not let them go.

Sorting through the gods he'd heard about, looking for one to pray to, he decided none would help. If he listened hard, he could hear their laughter.

They had awakened a beast. It was going to be a long night.

———

BETH SPENT the next morning running in front of the warriors. She was closer to home than she'd thought. The trail was familiar and she learned two things. The first was that she was in better shape, and could run faster than the warriors. That was important because they were unable to run around her to set up their own ambush. One tried and earned an arrow in his thigh for his trouble. The other thing of importance she learned was that the quiver of arrows she picked up from the camp were made of green wood, not dried reeds. That's why the warrior trying to get around her was shot in the thigh. She'd aimed at his gut. The arrows flew like a dove trying to dodge a falcon.

She was close enough to Jones Mill that she knew she could beat the warriors to safety. She'd promised Big Hand one more trick and she intended to use it. She'd lead them through Big Bramble. Just over the hill black-berries had taken over a small valley. In season, the locals would go there to pick the fruit—along with bears, raccoons and any other creature that could reach them. Everyone stayed around the outside. The brambles were ages old, tough and razor sharp. Since it was filled with rabbits, it was a good place to hunt. Providing you knew a way through.

The bad thing about the bramble was it didn't look so bad at first. In the spring, the vines were pliable and soft. You could deal with them. With the heat of the summer, the vines became hard and unforgiving. Along the perimeter, the bramble was covered with wild clematis and honeysuckle. It made a wall that hid the center. Once inside, you couldn't turn around without hanging up on thorns. A small person could navigate through without too much pain. Usually.

Once over the hill, she hesitated at the start of the bramble long enough for them to see her. She sent an arrow their way. There was no hope of hitting them, but she hoped to fuel their anger. Turning, she walked into the bramble. At the start she could move normally if she used a slow pace. Hearing the footfalls behind her, she hurried forward and then dropped to her hands and knees. She carried her bow and quiver in her hands. Anything on her back would hang up in the thorns above. Knowing the risk of getting hung up on the vines, she was especially careful with her hair. There was no sense in capturing herself.

Halfway through the vine-choked valley, she heard a shriek behind her. One of the men was caught and thrashing against the vines. It was the worst thing he could do and only produced a bloodletting. She could hear the other men shouting at the man to be still, but it didn't sound like he was listening.

The dry-bean warning of an angry rattlesnake stopped her in mid-crawl. Coiled a few steps in front of her, it was probably looking for the same rabbits she used to hunt. Fat and angry, the large snake guarded the path she needed to take. If she waited, it probably would go on its way. But she didn't have that kind of time.

She rose to her knees and slapped it down with the tip of her bow. It took a few tries to stun it and then get the bow under the snake. There was just enough of an opening above to flip the snake several yards behind her. It was stunned now, but when it woke it would be mad and looking for payback. With a feral smile, she hurried toward the edge of the bramble.

Minutes later she walked out of Big Bramble into the shade of the forest. Bleeding from scratches, gasping from the heat and exertion of crawling through the maze of thorny undergrowth, she took several deep breaths to calm herself.

Behind her, about three-fourths of the way through, muttered cursing and occasional shaking of vines marked the passage of the warriors struggling through the small valley. They'd finally dropped down to crawl, but were still too big and impatient to avoid the thorns.

Her shout was a mixture of French, English and Osage. "Big Hand. I stole some arrows from your camp. It is not right to steal so I'm going to return them now."

Beth shot all the arrows into the area where she'd last seen evidence of their passage. She was shooting blind because she couldn't see them. When she ran out of arrows, she threw down the quiver and faced the forest. It was decision time. The killing blood still ran high in her veins. It was a risk to steal more arrows from the renegade camp, and she could do little with her knife. It would serve her better to go to Jones Mill and re-supply.

Having made her decision, she gave one last look at the struggling warriors. Giving the keening war cry of the Osage, she shook her bow at them in defiance. Ever mindful of the surrounding forest, she turned and jogged toward home.

# Chapter Seventeen

ELLEN GAZED OUT THE SMALL WINDOW OF HER kitchen, trying to decide if closing the shutters would keep out the heat or trap it inside. She didn't know how long she'd stood trying to make such a mundane decision, but judging by the twisted and ripped towel in her hand it had been a while.

How could she be so stupid? Why did she keep driving Sean away? It was never her intention. And now he thought she'd been fooling around with that pompous ass Ambrose? Any fooling around was in his mind only and while not glad he was dead—it didn't upset her much. Her shame was that Sean had to kill the man because of her. What had her life become?

So, where to go from here? With Beth well on her way to Saint Louis and Sean always out in the forest, she was alone with her thoughts. Lately, that had not been a good thing.

Looking around her cabin, she was again ashamed. Like most inside the post it was built against the protective walls. But Sean had expanded rooms sideways, giving them two bedrooms, a great room, and kitchen and even an enclosed breezeway to the outhouse. While she complained, he'd taken great pains to fill the cracks between the logs of the home making it tight against the cold of winter. He'd even wrangled planks from the mill for a wood floor. While most homes sported a single fireplace, she had a large cast-iron stove in the kitchen used for cooking and heat in the winter. She had no idea where he'd found it or how he'd packed it in. He'd just shrugged and smiled.

When she gazed in the mirror hanging next to the kitchen door, it reflected an image she didn't like. The realization was like cold water poured over her. She'd spent most of a year trying to be something she was not. And for what?

She was afraid. Afraid for herself and Beth. And yes, for Sean. It seemed every time he came back from his jaunts into the forest, he had a fresh scar to show for the adventure.

Pulling her hands over her face, she shrugged at her reflection in the mirror. With Beth safe, she needed to show a backbone. She loved Sean and knew he loved her. It was time to show it. A few moments later, she'd changed clothes and packed away the frilly dresses that symbolized a woman she no longer wanted to be.

The scuffling of feet on her porch brought her around.

In a hopeful voice, she asked. "Sean?"

"No, ma'am. It's Colonel Thompson and Shay."

She stepped out under the awning. "Hello, Shay. What can I do for you, Colonel?"

"Well," the colonel replied. "We're going around to everyone enlisting help. I just returned from a homestead that was wiped out. Trouble may be headed our way."

Hands clutched to her stomach, he looked at Sean's friend. "Who were they?"

"I don't think you knew them. They were new to the area, I only met them a couple of times. From what I understand, it was very bad there. We'll need all the help we can get," he paused to grin at her, "I may have mentioned to the colonel how good a shot you are."

Shay edged away a moment fearful of her cutting voice, and then stopped. Another slow smile dawned on his face. "Wait a minute. The clothes you're wearing. Is the old Ellen back?"

"Yes, Shay." She chuckled, feeling unbelievable relief. "The old Ellen is back. I've killed the new one and hidden the body under the porch."

Colonel Thompson stared between the two and then at the boards at his feet. "I'm not sure..."

"Relax, Colonel." Her hand touched his arm. "We're just joking. I'm ready and willing to help defend the post. I'll be alongside my husband when he returns. Have you seen him?"

"Your husband?" Shay interrupted. "When did that happen?"

She gazed at him with an arched eyebrow and pointed look. "I think we've been together long enough for that to be the case, don't you?"

"Oh, yes, ma'am. I surely do." Shay gave her a knowing glance. "Does he know he's trapped yet?"

Uncertainty tainted her voice. "He'll know soon enough and he's well past the honeymoon stage."

The colonel cleared his throat for attention. "Please, if I may continue. He's a good man, your husband. I think he's scouting around with that Indian woman—"

"Stands Tall," Shay interrupted.

"—to see what we're up against. He shouldn't be far behind us."

"A woman?" Ellen's voice was sharp.

"I've seen her around the post. Oh, she's a beautiful one." Shay's dancing eyes watched her with interest. "I've heard she's a medicine woman. They do claim she can cast a spell if need be and yet...has no husband."

"Well, she'd better..." She caught Shay's expression. "Dammit, Shay. Stop pulling my strings. I'm having a hard enough time without you egging me on."

"But Ellen." He smiled at her. "It's what I live for. There are few enough distractions for us during the day."

Colonel Thompson held his hand up between them. "It looks like we're done here. As soon as Mr. MacLeod returns, we'll have a better idea of what we face. Please look to your weapons and ammunition. If you need extra powder and ball, please come and see me. We have plenty."

The colonel gestured toward another cabin. "Shay? If you please?"

She watched them walk away. Looking through the gate and beyond the walls she could see soldiers moving to the outlying cabins, she supposed to warn people and bring them into the post. The place would be crowded for a few days. Sighing, she went back inside. She hadn't practiced with her rifle in a long time. Sean took care of the hunting...or Beth.

Beth. Ellen reached into a corner to retrieve her rifle and see to the priming. At least Beth was safe and on her way to a new life.

# Chapter Eighteen

Sean stepped into the forest surrounding the McGill's homestead, crossing the stream where he'd found the scuff mark on the slick limestone. The hard-wood canopy filtered the sunshine, darkening the moss-covered deadfalls and sides of the trees. A faint deer tail led around the hill.

He turned to Stands Tall, following close behind. "From now on, we need to be silent. Can you do that?"

She stared at him until he chuckled. "Well, I guess you can."

Her voice was soft. "I'm no child in the forest."

He was hesitant to do this. Although putting on like she was a female warrior, she was still his responsibility. After seeing what happened to the women at McGill's, he didn't want to take any more risks than was necessary.

"I'll be looking for sign, which will keep my head down. I want you to travel behind me, with your head up and eyes on the forest. Don't let us walk into an ambush."

"Of course." Her voice turned sarcastic. "My people have been doing this for all remembered time."

He stared at her a moment before moving up the trail. There was little to see. But the trail was there. A broken twig on dense sumac, overturned sticks or rocks showing their dark side up instead of down, or more scuff marks in the soft trail. A lot of it was choosing a path that would afford the least amount of trouble and noise. The warriors weren't taking much care about hiding their passage, which worried him.

Their pursuit was disjointed and slow, pausing often to decide if they were trailing someone or finding things that naturally occur when animals use the trail. They'd seen no bear or large deer so Sean felt they weren't wasting their time. Glancing at the sun, he was sure they weren't much farther from Jones Mill than they had been at McGills.

"Stop." Her voice was a low whisper.

Sean froze in place and looked around the forest. "What is it?"

"I hear crying."

He gave her an exasperated look. "All I hear are crows and magpies."

With a snort, she led the way around the hill in front of them.

He hurried to follow, instinctively taking the position of being a sentinel for her. "Careful. It could be a trap."

The small clearing they found was typical of an Indian camp. A lot of space wasn't needed, with a lean-to made of poles and a bark roof to give their horses some shelter. The large deer-hide tepee sat next to it with a cooking fire outside the entrance. The dwelling had slash marks and holes in it. The attack must have been a surprise because nobody would use a hide tent to make a last stand.

Stands Tall hesitated and then walked to the edge of

the clearing to bring back a baby, wrapped in blankets. "The mother must have hidden the baby when the attack came."

Sean shrugged, still gazing at the forest. "Maybe. More likely, she was out picking berries or something when she heard the attack. Laid the baby down and rushed to help. It's a story we'll never know."

She rocked the baby, trying to get it quiet. "Is the mother inside?"

He shook his head. "That's the bad news on top of bad news. She must be captive." He pointed with his chin toward the forest. "Or she's out there somewhere."

"We need to get this baby to Jones Mill or the Cherokee settlement and find someone nursing. She's hungry."

Glancing at the fat baby, he poked at it through the blankets. "It doesn't look like she's starving. Hopefully you can quiet her." Sean looked around one more time. "I've seen enough, so we may as well go. With the lungs on that child, there's no use trying to be quiet."

The pounding of feet on the trail was the only warning. A brave launched through the air with a shrill cry, swinging his tomahawk at Sean's head. Dropping to the ground, Sean avoided the blow and came up holding his fighting knife. Another brave walked into the clearing, looking at Stands Tall and the baby.

The warrior with the tomahawk moved toward Sean. "It's good we stayed behind. Now we have a white man to kill and another woman for our pleasure."

Sean shook his head. "I wouldn't count on that."

The man raised his tomahawk for an overhand blow, looking to end the fight with a mighty, impressive strike. But there is no strength in an arm pointed straight up. Sean stepped in and blocked the warrior's arm, coming up with his knife into the man's belly. The Indian tried to deflect the knife with his other hand but was too slow. Sean's strike was quick and brutal and meant to be because there were two more of them.

Surprised the others hadn't joined the fight, he turned to find them running away down the trail and then dodging into the brush. Grabbing the bow he'd dropped, he notched an arrow and waited. A few seconds later, one of the men appeared, looking back at them. Like a fleeing deer, once they think they're out of danger, they always turn to look. Men and animals weren't much different.

The fleeing Indian would have been out of range for a normal bow, but Sean's longbow sent the metal-tipped arrow through the man's chest. The warrior took a surprised look to his death. The other warrior didn't appear.

Trying to control his breathing, he turned and gawked at Stands Tall. She seemed unconcerned.

"You seem angry." She watched him carefully as she yawned, her voice neutral. "Why should I have been worried? They were simple warriors. I have the Ghostrider for protection."

"Yeah, but don't count on it. There were three of them. If two hadn't run, it was going to get interesting. And I'm getting tired of finding bodies and being the target of every raggedy-assed hostile we see."

She snorted, rocking the baby on her shoulder. "Well you made up for it."

"For these. Only for these." It bothered him that they hadn't found the woman, but he knew if she was alive, she'd have been with her baby. Or captured. That looked to be a fate much worse than death.

Walking to the first Indian he'd killed, Stands Tall looked and hissed, "Shawnee."

As they moved up the trail again, she paused at the other man. "I don't know this one. Maybe Mohawk? What would they be doing here?"

"I don't know." Sean looked around. "We better make tracks to get to the fort by nightfall. We have much to do."

# Chapter Nineteen

THEY'D PASSED THROUGH THE PRAIRIES AND ROLLING hills of western Missouri, traveling south into the foothills of the borderland that led to Arkansas. It wasn't a gentle transition. Their journey turned more circum-spect, dominated by hills to ride around and many more streams to cross. There wasn't a straight line to anywhere.

Jim Walker rode in front of their little cavalcade with his rifle across the saddle. Knowing the country and what he was getting into, they stopped at a trading post on the Neosho River, little more than a mud and bark-covered shack at a junction of trails. There was a canvas tent pitched behind it. He figured that was the living quarters because the porous building in front of him was too frail to stop a whistle, much less a cold wind. Looking at a hand-written sign hung from a post, he was surprised at the variety of goods offered. All he'd stopped to trade was his rifle. He hated to part with it, but the country they were coming to provided little chance for long-range shooting.

Dismounting and holding his rifle, he glanced at the men slouched around the front door of the post. An unkempt and motley looking pair, they sat in mismatched buckskins and muslin guarded by an old dog too lazy to wag a greeting. Jim smiled. Both women had their rifles pointed at the men and they seemed a little antsy.

The proprietor came to the door and held out his hand for greeting. "No need to be skittish, Mister. Your women can put their guns away. My name's Miller Nesbitt. Can I interest you in something?"

Jim shook the hand offered with distaste and nodded, giving the man a wary look. "Jim Walker, and I figure those rifles are resting easy. These ladies didn't reach maturity by being trusting of folks."

One of the men turned his head and spit, snorting a laugh. He started to rise and Angry Woman booted her horse closer before she spoke. "Sit."

Jim could almost smile at what the men were looking at. Two women, both with children strapped in a pouch against their chests, horses loaded with possible bags and blankets—the reins of pack horses tied to their saddles. And two very businesslike rifles pointed right at them. The bores of those rifles must have looked like cave openings.

Miller took a step backward with an uneasy chuckle. "That woman looks angry. What'd you do to her?"

He was starting to see an advantage of bringing that particular sister along. "Nothing. She's been that way since I've known her. I think she's had a bad experience with menfolk."

The trader gave her a long look before turning back to Jim. "Well, if you ain't here to be sociable, what can I do for you?"

"I'm looking to trade my rifle for a shorter-barreled musket. I figure that would be more useful in the brush country south of here."

The man smiled. "I might can help you with that. C'mon inside. You got any money?"

Not liking the dark interior of the building, he responded with a shrug. "Reckon I'll be just fine out here."

"If I might ask, where ya headed?"

Jim hesitated a minute, staring at the man. He didn't get the feeling the man was crooked, but he'd been fooled by friendly faces before. "Headed down to Jones Mill. Sean MacLeod is a friend of mine and is supposed to be around there."

Miller gave him a surprised look. "You just missed him. He was through here about three weeks ago. He's thinking about taking up some land east of here."

"I'll catch up with him pretty soon, then." He smirked at his own joke. "I have a delivery for him."

"You might be interested in some new rifles that arrived a couple of days ago." He ducked inside and brought out a shorter length rifle. "This here's called a Hall Rifle. It's a breech loader. Once you get used to it, and you have the proper ammunition and fixin's, you can fire about six shots a minute. It'll take the same ball as your Kentucky Rifle. That's right helpful in some situations."

The man proceeded to show him how the barrel hinged open toward the back. "See? You don't have to use a long stick to seat the ball and the actual barrel stays clean. You don't have black powder building up in the rifling. It's a purty good gun."

"Mister Nesbitt, you just made a sale. I'll take three

and trade in my rifles. I just bought two of them new at Chouteau's Post at Kawsmouth. Did you talk Sean into one of these?"

"Nope, didn't have them when he was here."

"What's the best way to Jones Mill?"

"Just keep heading south. The next river of any size will be the White. Follow it downstream until you see the Mill. Can't miss it."

"How will we know it's the right river?"

"All the rivers and creeks around here are warm. The one you want is so cold you need to find a shallow ford to cross. If you get in too deep of water, you'll lose your balls —they'll freeze right off." The man leaned on the new rifle he was trading. "That is, of course, if the fish don't get them first. They're large enough to feed your family for a day."

"Uh-huh." Jim shook his head. "I'll put that information right next to all the other tall tales I've heard. How long will it take?"

"The trip? Another day and a half to Jones Mill. Your balls? I figure they will be gone in about a minute once you hit that water."

Jim took a bag off his horse while Fawn raised an eyebrow at him, stifling a smile. "I think we've discussed the loss of my manhood long enough. Let's go inside and settle up."

He paused a moment, holding the man's gaze with his own. "I'm going to be plumb disappointed if there's anyone inside waiting for us."

Miller shook his head. "You can rest easy. Can I gather those other rifles and look them over?"

Making eye contact with Fawn, he inclined his head toward the men. She gave a curt nod. "Oh, I think the rifles will be just fine where they are, at least until we're ready to leave. I'm going to trust you but I don't know about those men."

The dark interior of the building was filled with pelts, mostly beaver and muskrat. Two planks stretched across flour barrels served as a counter. A small scale sat in the center, just in case gold or silver was used.

After a few minutes of discussing what was needed and haggling over price, they heard a shout from outside. "*Vous Arrettez*. Stop."

A gunshot punctuated the order to stop.

Rushing outside, they found Angry Woman pointing the smoking barrel of her rifle at a man slumped over on the ground, a red blossom of blood spreading on his back from the .40 caliber ball. The other man, still sitting on the bench, had his hands in the air. His eyes had widened impossibly large while he gulped for air. The stain on the front of his trousers spread, along with the smell. The lazy dog rose, gave them a jaundiced eye, and walked a few feet away before plopping down with a sigh.

Jim relaxed, seeing everything was under control. "What happened?"

Fawn shrugged, her rifle pointing at the remaining man while Angry Woman reloaded hers. "That man started telling what they would do to us after we left. He said they'd catch up with us and kill you. Then they would have us and all our supplies. I tried to shut him up but he wouldn't listen. Angry Woman has little patience for that."

Jim glanced at the proprietor, shaking his head. "Nor do I."

Nesbitt shrugged, giving the impression he didn't care but didn't meet Jim's gaze. "They're just hangers-on, always looking for free whiskey. No skin off my nose."

The shooting seemed to motivate the storekeeper as

he moved quickly around the dim interior. When they were through, Jim emerged with three of the new rifles, a twenty-pound bag of brown beans and a bag of peaches. He'd sorted through the peaches inside to pick the best ones. Loading the rifles under the watchful eye of Miller Nesbitt, he handed one to each of the women. When they took the new rifles, it was the first time he'd seen Angry Woman smile. It'd taken a lot of gold to make that happen but might be worth it in the long run.

When he took their old guns, Jim unloaded each of them before laying them on the ground. He looked over at the man keeping an uncomfortable vigil on their log bench, next to the dead body. Wrinkling his nose, he turned to Miller.

"I'll be right disappointed if we find anyone on our back trail. If that happens, I'll be back to see you. Personal."

"I swear." Miller shook his head. "You're about the most untrusting folks I ever seen."

"I find that hard to believe." Jim snorted. "Who knows? Maybe next time we'll stay and chat, break open a jug of flip or something."

"Sounds fine, Mister Walker. Just don't bring that one gal with ya. She scares the pants off me. I've seen bears in rutting season friendlier than her."

They rode south about a mile, pulled into the trees and waited. After he was sure no one followed, he dismounted. "Let's spread a blanket and let the little ones rest and play awhile. We need to practice loading these new rifles until we're good at it and then go on down the trail. If we camp in a few hours, I figure that'll put us in at Jones Mill a little after noon tomorrow."

Fawn looked at Angry Woman a moment before

speaking. "We are rich with supplies and horses. It will be good to be somewhere protected. Many people would kill us for what we have."

He nodded, glancing around at the forest. "Why do you think I have you practicing with your rifles? But if it comes to a choice, don't try to save the pack animals. The most important thing to save is yourselves and the children. Nothing else is more important."

She hugged him a moment and then spoke to her sister. "See? Good man. Much different than old ways."

He smirked at Angry Woman as she snorted and turned away. He thought a smile started on her face, but couldn't be sure. If it bothered her that she'd just killed a man, it didn't show.

They practiced loading the Hall rifles, including getting used to seating the small percussion caps. Jim hadn't used them before, being used to flint for igniting the powder. Only two of them practiced at a time, with the third watching the forest around them.

The children played and rolled around on a blanket while chewing on deer jerky. He wondered how long it would be before they weaned. Sparrow was just learning to walk. Little Sean kept wandering away and had to be herded back often, being too curious for his own good.

Finally satisfied with the practice loading, he had everyone mount and the little caravan moved south again. He'd would have liked to carry his daughter, but wanted to be ready for trouble. He'd worried about the people behind him since leaving Chouteau's Post, and especially since leaving Miller Nesbitt's store. Hopefully, that worry would end soon.

His mood suddenly turned festive. As anxious as he was to get to the relative safety of the settlement, he was even more anxious to see the look on Sean's face. He couldn't stop a chuckle, drawing a head shake and exasperated look from Fawn. They'd talked of it before and she probably knew what he was thinking.

He nudged his horse forward with his heels. He could hardly wait. This was going to be good.

# Chapter Twenty

IT WAS LATE AFTERNOON WHEN SEAN AND STANDS Tall walked through the gate of Jones Mill. The first person they encountered was Anais Thorn. Coattails flapping, he skidded to a dusty stop staring at them and the foundling baby.

The preacher's voice carried over the compound. "You couldn't stop with your adulterous ways? Now you've brought another woman and your spawn with you? Have you no shame?"

Sean was a step toward the man with his knife half out of its scabbard when he felt a hand on his arm. He looked down, surprised to see Ellen shaking her head at him. "Please don't kill him. He's a fool and should be suffered as such."

He stared hard at the man, but finally relaxed under Ellen's touch. "No, he's An-ass. If he doesn't shut up his insults, I'm going to put him down."

She patted his arm before turning and facing the minister. "Please leave us."

With a nasal harrumph and a twist of the bullet riddled coat tail, the preacher stalked away.

No one approached the couple, although people must have expected fireworks because they watched from the shade of porches and from behind curtains. Did they think he couldn't see that curtain moving? He guessed he couldn't blame them. A good part of them seldom left the confines of the settlement. There were few enough distractions for them in an otherwise boring existence. He could never understand why they moved to this place if they remained so afraid they wouldn't leave the walls.

Ellen spoke, watching the preacher until he was out of earshot. Her hand still clutched his forearm as she gave a glance at the Indian woman holding the infant. "Your friend is very beautiful. Is this the famous Stands Tall?"

For a moment he didn't know what to say. Once again, she'd changed. Gone were the dresses and accoutrement of the gentle living style she'd professed to want when he left a few days ago. This was the Ellen he remembered and loved. Dressed in buckskin, tanned almost white, her hair was pulled back and fastened with a red ribbon. Realizing he still wanted to be with her and that she was trying to come back, he tried to defend himself.

"Yes, and she's a good friend." He turned and grinned at Stands Tall. "Depending on who you ask, she's either a healer or a witch."

Ellen extended her hand, keeping Sean between them. "Then she's a friend of mine."

The two women clasped their hands, although Stands Tall seemed a little uncomfortable with the white man's custom. Sean interrupted the awkward moment. "On the way back from trying to find out who killed the settlers, we found this baby outside a camp destroyed by the Shawnee. The parents are dead and we're hoping to find someone in the Cherokee village to nurse the baby—maybe adopt her."

Ellen rubbed her finger over the baby's cheek. "Oh, I believe you. Don't be so defensive. I see nothing of you in her." She scrutinized Stands Tall. "Or, of you. We can take her to our cabin. I've seen the Osage use a bladder made of gut to give babies goat's milk, or cow's milk, if we can't find a wet-nurse. We'd just have to dilute it with water."

Sean looked at her. We? Well, she was always quick to help. At least, before.... He gave her a curious look. "Ellen, you seem to have come back from the dead."

Before Ellen could form a reply, Stands Tall started to leave. "Thank you, Ellen. But you have bigger problems than this. Tend to your man. I'll see if I can find someone nursing from the Cherokee village. That would be the better way. Someone there may know the family that was killed. If not...the baby will not go hungry for long."

She gave Sean a direct look. "Remember what I told you, Ghostrider? Walk around the tree."

Ellen gave Stands Tall a long, curious look as the woman moved away. "Well, that's strange advice."

A loud voice carrying across the compound interrupted them. "I'm looking for a no-account fraud of a mountain man called Ghostrider—got a reputation for running away from every Blackfoot he ever saw. He's probably hiding under a blanket somewhere. Anyone seen Sean MacLeod around here?"

They turned to see a tall man dressed in buckskins and a floppy, gray hat. Behind him two Indian women held squirming children and rifles at the ready, while leading a couple of pack mules full of supplies—something few people could accomplish. The man kept riding toward them with a big grin on his face while the women stopped just inside the gates, taking up positions that would guard the exit if they had to fight their way out. The expressions of the women reflected the surprise shown by the people standing around the buildings.

"Sean?" Ellen's voice came soft next to him, as she clutched his arm. "Who...do you know this man?"

Sean laughed, seeing people start to gather around, before replying in a loud voice. "Folks, this old broken-down excuse for a trapper is Jim Walker. The only beaver he ever caught were floating face down on the water, dead of old age. Last I saw of him, he was sneaking out the back of a tepee without his pants." He made a show of leaning over to look at the two women near the gate. "Looks like he got caught."

Always ready for some entertainment, the people around them guffawed.

"You only saw me because you were ahead of me, looking back." The man came off his horse and strode toward Sean. A few moments later they were pounding each other on their shoulders and sporting wide grins.

Sean turned to Ellen and Stands Tall who'd stopped to watch. "This broken-down old mountain man is a friend of mine. It's been what...a year and a half?"

"Almost two." Jim nodded, waving the women at the gate forward. "A lot of water down the river in that amount of time. Yessir, a lot of water."

His grin threatened to split his face as he glanced back toward the two approaching women. "Remember Chouteau's Post? Man, that was a time, wasn't it? You came out of the forest looking so much like a drowned rat that I had to take you under my wing and help."

Sean's neck turned red. "Yeah, I remember. It was a

pretty good time." He quickly put his arm around Ellen. "That was before I met Ellen."

Jim's grin threatened to split his face before he nodded. "Yeah, I expect it was. Well, no matter. Look who I found when I came back through Chouteau's." One of the women dismounted and came forward. "This is Fawn. Remember her? And this is our little daughter, Sparrow."

He hit Sean on the shoulder and laughed, not able to hide the pride in his voice. "I've got a daughter. Ain't she something?"

"And a wife, it seems." Ellen's voice held relief. "Or, two?"

"Well, nothing formal, but she is my wife. That's true. When a wife has sisters, sometimes you inherit one." Jim glanced at Sean. "But not always. Remember Willow, Fawn's daughter?"

Jim spoke softly to Ellen in a stage whisper. "Willow was very attentive to Sean when we were at Chouteau's Post."

"Yeah. I remember." Sean's reply was guarded while he craned his neck, looking at the other woman with some relief. "And that's not her."

Jim nodded; his expression turned serious. "You're right. That is not her. It's sad to report that Willow died. But bad as that was, she left a little remembrance for you."

After waiting a moment and getting no explanation, Sean shook his head in exasperation and glanced at Fawn. "I'm sorry, Fawn. She was a sweet girl."

Fawn nodded and he couldn't understand why she was smiling. Her daughter's death could not have been a joke.

At a gesture from Jim, the other woman came forward, carrying a child. She took the boy from her carry-pouch and sat him on the ground. He immediately struggled to his feet, staring around at them. Even at his young age, his size and strength were evident.

Reactions were immediate. Ellen gasped and Stands Tall giggled at the same time.

Jim made a flourishing move toward the boy. "Sean, I'd like you to meet...Sean Junior."

Sean stood in shock a moment, remembering his conversation with Buffalo Horn, Willow's grandfather. They'd agreed that he'd be told if Willow had a child. No word had come to him and Buffalo Horn was a man of his word. "How? No. Not possible."

"Well, I'm pretty sure you know how." Ellen strode forward, ignoring the angry looking woman trying to block her way. She picked the squirming boy up and held him at arm's length. "And it certainly looks possible to me. Dammit, Sean. Everyone here can see he's yours. He's..." She seemed at a loss for words a moment before finishing in a soft voice. "He's perfect."

"Well, I don't know about perfect." Jim laughed. "But you gotta admit there ain't too many blue-eyed Nez Percé around."

They all stood in a rough circle. Jim introduced Angry Woman as Fawn's sister before commenting. "Dammit, boy. I'm just plum disappointed. I was going to have a lot better time introducing you to your son. Been looking forward to it ever since I saw him. This is kind of a letdown. Why so glum? It can't be that big of a disaster. I thought you'd be proud."

Sean watched Ellen holding the boy, talking quietly to the other women, including Stands Tall who'd rejoined the group. He shook his head in wonder. Ellen had taken instant possession of him.

"Seems like a damned lot of babies around here all of

a sudden," Sean said. "Not sure how to take it all. And it's a bad time to try and get my head around something like this. We got trouble here, Jim. Big trouble."

"Aw, come on, Sean. It can't be that much of a surprise. Besides, the womenfolk mostly take care of the babies. All we have to do is play with them and spoil them a bit."

"That isn't the trouble I'm talking about."

He was about to tell of the killings when Ellen came over and handed the boy to him. "Take your son, Sean."

The boy reached for him and came naturally to his arms. As they stared at each other, they touched foreheads. That was all it took for Ellen to start crying as she stood by his side.

"I want him, Sean. He's part of you and that makes him family. He has to stay with us. Jim and his ladies too. We're all family now."

"Oh? So we're a family again?" Noting her firm expression, he conceded. "I agree. All are welcome here. I'm all for that, but it may not be so easy. There is something bad going on."

"What's happened?" Jim interjected, finally putting on his serious face. "We met some folks headed north on our way here and they gave us wide berth. They didn't stop to talk and acted real nervous."

Sean nodded. "There's an unknown party of Indians, mostly Shawnee we think, passing through our land. Don't know how many yet, but by the sign they left I'm guessing around forty. They've killed some people and what they do to the women is unspeakable."

"What do you mean?"

Stands Tall interrupted. "They cut off their breasts after raping and killing them." Her voice lowered. "At least, we pray it's after."

Jim glanced at his women and then closed his eyes a moment before shaking his head and sighing. "We've seen that before, up north. It ain't common though."

Sean nodded. "We don't know who they are or why they're doing it, but we need to stop them."

"I can help with that." The new voice, strained and hoarse, froze them a moment. "There's only about twenty of them left and they're not far behind me—mad as hornets."

At first, when they turned to look, the speaker appeared to be a young man with torn and bloody clothes, bent over at the waist and gasping from running hard.

Ellen's hand came to her mouth before she screamed. "Beth? Oh my God. Beth!"

Beth dropped her bow and empty quiver before Ellen slammed into her with open arms, nearly crushing her in a hug. Although a full head shorter than her daughter, she pulled her off her feet. A few moments later, Beth raised her head from her mother's shoulder and looked at Sean with haunted eyes. To him, they showed a maturity far beyond her age. He knew at a glance those eyes had seen things no girl her age should have.

He looked behind her, waiting for anyone else coming through the gate. Turning his attention to her, his gaze sharpened. This was a different Beth—not the young adolescent girl that left with Buffalo Shield. A momentary sadness hit him. He didn't know what the particulars were, he'd learn that later. But one look and he knew she'd been hardened and shaped by the fire of conflict. It was a fire you survived, or died in.

Her adopted grandfather wasn't with her, and only one thing would cause that. He'd already resigned himself to it, but had to ask. "Buffalo Shield?"

Beth met his gaze and shook her head. Her look was grim, pinching back tears. Sean sighed. His shoulders slumped a moment before squaring with purpose. The why of it would come later. But it didn't matter right now. Her bloody clothes and exhausted expression were testimony enough. She was young for it, but returned to her family as a full-fledged member of a society called warriors.

"He died well?"

She shook her head. "I wasn't there for it. I'd say he died hard."

He rolled that through his mind a moment, finally deciding it didn't matter. "Are you followed?"

"Probably." Her shrug was expressive. "More than likely. Those Shawnee don't like me much."

Sean nodded. "Ellen, please take everyone to our cabin. I'm sure they need to freshen up after their trip and get something to eat and drink. All these babies probably need fed."

When he put his hand on her, he intended to get her attention. Instead, Ellen released her daughter and came into his arms. This new compliant behavior was something new and unexpected—maybe. Babies make women do unexpected things.

His warning voice was soft in her ear. "Be careful, Ellen. We don't know what has happened, but this isn't the same daughter that left. She's been through a lot and grown up suddenly. Don't crowd her."

"You're giving me advice on my own daughter?" Her smile belied her mocking tone. "I understand, Sean. Believe me, I do. But she still needs her mother. We can get reacquainted. I'm sure we don't need you men around for that."

He nodded and let her go, turning to his friend. "Jim,

there's a stable next to the soldier's office. You can unload your pack animals there. No one will bother anything." He pointed toward Shay's tavern connected to the store. "When you're done, meet us over at the tavern."

"No." Beth struggled against her mother. "Sean. Please. We need to talk. There is..."

He held his hand up. "We will. I don't think the danger is immediate, or we'd be combing musket balls out of our hair right now. Let your mother fuss over you awhile, get you cleaned up and see to your injuries if you're hurt. Then all of you come to the tavern. I'm sure there are some stories here that we all need to hear."

As they parted, Beth suddenly faced Stands Tall. Both of equal height, they stood within inches of each other. Beth did not flinch away, but calmly watched the older woman. Stands Tall, eyes narrowed as she inspected the young girl suddenly gasped, bringing a hand to her heart.

"I see." Shaking her head in wonder, she whispered. "Mishipeshu! Can it be?"

"That's a name the Shawnee called me, but I don't know the true meaning of it. If it means anger, I understand. I have so much of that it burns my heart." Beth reached out to her, clutching her arm. Her voice was soft. "I am your friend."

With a huge grin plastered on her face Stands Tall hugged her, shifting the foundling baby to her hip and then draping an arm around the girl's shoulder as they followed the other women to Ellen's cabin.

Standing with his mouth open, Sean watched them walk away. Three babies and all those women under one roof? Nothing good could come from that. He shook his head as they walked away. "Mishi...what?"

Shaking his head, thinking women were beyond his ken, he turned away. He'd been watching the soldiers while he talked. Striding quickly over to their building, he spoke to the commandant. "Colonel Thompson, I have news that the party of Indians causing the trouble are close. You need to set sentries and quick. I don't know what's going on, but it can't be good. Ring the bell to bring in outlying settlers. We may be attacked soon."

"Thanks for the word." After a quick glance toward the forest, the colonel gave a short nod, yelling orders as he turned back into the building.

Hands on hips, Sean took a giant breath and let it out slow. Jim joined him as they moved toward the tavern.

"Well, that got things moving in a damned big hurry." Jim's smile was infectious.

Sean glanced at him, knowing they had much to talk about. "You're through unpacking? That didn't take long."

Jim laughed and clapped him on the shoulder. "Man over there said he'd take care of it."

He gave a curious glance at the stable. "You got money for that?"

"Sure I do. Well, actually...you do. I'll be glad to stand for drinks and explain all that."

"That would be nice, especially if you buy them with my money." Sean glanced toward Ellen's cabin. "You can start with telling me about my son."

# Chapter Twenty-One

STONEFACE STALKED AROUND THE CLEARING AND campsite. The bodies of the fallen had been dragged into the forest, but the wind shifted and they were already beginning to smell. The scavengers of the forest would have a feast. And how could this happen? He could understand losing men in a battle with other warriors. It was expected. But this? So many dead from one little girl. Maybe his men were right. Maybe she was *Mishipeshu*. His gaze took in the warriors gathered around the fire. The numbers were dwindling and the warriors left would hardly look at him.

One of his men brought him some venison. He ate, absentmindedly noting it was a tough piece, his mind on the forest and the problems he faced. Without building up his force, there was little hope of terrorizing the settlers to get them to move. When looking at the problem, there was little point to that now. Any riches promised had died with Ambrose. The Army officer had lied to him. There were more tribes here than he'd been told, and many more people.

The Osage would be coming home from their buffalo hunt soon and only a fool fought the Osage. He could continue going west with his men with no shame, a choice that would appeal to them as well. Except for the girl.

Big Hand should have returned and was overdue. How long could it take to capture and kill one female and bring his trophies?

At a muted whistle from one of his warriors, he looked where the man pointed. Big Hand and his men emerged from the forest and strode toward him. As they approached, Stoneface stood with his mouth open and felt his face flush with heat. He choked back a laugh that came out as a short bark.

The men were bleeding from cuts and scratches. None returned with their long rifles and two bows were missing. Big Hand had part of an arrow protruding from his shoulder. Another man had a grotesquely swollen face. A third warrior had an arrow wound in the thigh and was being supported by the two unwounded men.

The men stopped in a tight group, seeming to draw comfort from each other and unable to look at their leader. He expected to see anger and resentment. What he saw was defeat. These were beaten men. They would never be effective again.

Stoneface moved up to his second-in-command. "Were you ambushed by the Osage?"

"No."

"You found the girl?"

"We did." Big Hand grimaced as his leader tugged at the arrow shaft protruding from his shoulder.

Stoneface paused and made a show of looking around. "And yet I don't see her or my trophies. I'm sure there is a story to be heard?"

"We were close behind her." Big Hand continued. "She was running only fast enough to allow us to follow. We were led into a bad place and then the Night Panther found us. We'd followed her into a valley that looked to be choked in green vines over deadfalls of old trees. A giant wind must have gone through the valley sometime and blew them down. They were toppled everywhere. It looked like a good place for her to try and hide. We were right behind her and pushing hard, but we followed too fast. The outside of the valley was easy and we thought to catch her while she played the child's game of hiding. We did not know the middle was all thorns. I don't know how she got through to the other side."

"But she did." Stoneface had found a flat rock about the size of his hand. Drawing his arm back, he struck the arrow shaft, driving the point on through Big Hand's shoulder and punching out through the skin of his back. Once the head was out, he grabbed it and pulled it on through. Big Hand's knees buckled from the pain, but he stood stoically before his leader.

Breathing in gasps for a moment, Big Hand continued. "Once she got to the other side, she turned and shot arrows into us while we were trapped in the brambles." He shook his head. "There was no place to hide or get away."

"No place to hide from a little girl?" Nodding, Stoneface pointed his finger. "And this one? What happened to him?"

"She threw a rattlesnake on us while we were crawling through the brambles."

"This magical girl picked up a rattlesnake and threw it on him?" The man bitten by the rattlesnake rested on his knees, both hands cupping his face. His breathing was ragged and his eyes were swollen shut.

Stoneface folded his arms across his chest, flinching when they came to rest on the cut he'd inflicted to mimic the girl. "And the man with the arrow wound?"

Big Hand studied his leader's face a moment before speaking. "The point is lodged in his leg bone. We can't pull it out. I think the leg is broken."

He glanced at his second-in-command. "This is the second time you've failed me. I told you what would happen if you came back without her. Are you so ashamed by being defeated by a girl that you want to die? Do you want me to kill you?"

"I returned because you're running out of men." Big Hand shrugged, making a painful grimace. "I can still fight."

"Barely." Stoneface shook his head. "If you could still fight, you'd have brought the girl. But you're right about one thing. I'm running out of men. That's the only reason you're still alive." He pointed to the man with the leg wound and the other with the swollen face. "Kill these men. They are of no use to us. When you are finished, join me at the campfire. We must plan."

"Plan for what? We don't have enough men to attack the white man's settlement."

He watched Big Hand a moment. The man seemed different, not sure of himself—glancing at shadows and flinching at unexpected sounds. But when he thought about it, he was doing the same. Had one incident broken their backs?

Before, they'd seemed invincible as they moved from one attack to another. He'd planned every move so there would be little reprisal. Now? Someone, or something, had fought back and it surprised them. Was it simply a girl taken by a spirit? His men's eyes were drawn to the forest and fear painted their faces.

Big Hand voiced what was hidden in Stoneface's mind. "Why not continue toward the west. Surely there are easier kills for the men. They need women and rest. We all do."

He wasn't mad, he'd voiced it to himself before. Why not leave? It would be the prudent thing to do. "We cannot. We are men and have been insulted. The Whites must pay. The girl must pay. All this must be done before we move on."

Stoneface met the gaze of Big Hand until the man turned away. "We must draw them out and make them come to us. Once away from their protection, they belong to us. This is our time. We master the forest, not them."

Big Hand nodded and then jerked his gaze toward the fire when sap exploded from a green branch. He seemed embarrassed when he gave his attention back to Stoneface. "Where shall we dump the bodies?"

He stared at his second-in-command a moment, disappointed in him and not for the first time. He should be showing strength, not weakness. They'd come a long way together only to flounder in this forest. Was it full of bad spirits? Magical night panthers? He grunted and shook his head, fingering the arrow with the sharp, pointed head.

"Follow your nose, Big Hand. The pile of my fearless warriors is growing and rotting in the forest."

Moving toward the fire, Stoneface finally relaxed and let himself smile. The strong young girl consumed his thoughts. She would be caught. She would submit. Once that happened, he'd decide whether to kill her...or keep her.

In his mind, the Ghostrider was already dead. The

assault of their post would start in the morning while they slept.

# Chapter Twenty-Two

ELLEN USHERED HER NEW FRIENDS INTO HER HOME, stopping once at the threshold to turn and watch Sean striding toward the meeting place. His head was tilted to Jim Walker, listening to some comment. Little Sean squirmed, demanding her attention. Such a beautiful child.

The women waited patiently for her inside. Offering them places to sit, she handed the boy back to a surprised Angry Woman and set about organizing food and drink. Talking while she worked, bringing out bread and cheese, along with coffee and cream, their comments were freely flowing, with the help of Stands Tall.

She learned from Fawn that she and her sister were Nez Percé, a northern tribe forced south by the Black-foot and then the Sioux, finally stopping at Chouteau's Post. Their band was small. Since they'd learned the words of the Kansa and Sioux, both using the same language of the Osage, their conversations were a mix of French, English and native words accompanied by expressive use of their hands in sign language.

"We worked at Chouteau's Post," Fawn explained. "We were given rooms to live in and food if we helped in their great kitchen. They fed all who came to visit their post, at any time of the day or night."

Fawn paused a moment. "This will be confusing for you. Forgive my words if they have no meaning to you. My daughter Willow was not conceiving with her husband, and they wanted a child. Barren women are held in low esteem. When the Ghostrider appeared before us riding a great Nez Percé war horse, my father Buffalo Horn was much impressed. All our people had heard of this Ghostrider. My father decided when it was her fertile time, Willow should lay with him, thinking her husband had bad seed. If it didn't take, we would know she was barren. If it did, she would have a great warrior for a son."

"Or a daughter?" Beth interjected.

Fawn inclined her head. "Or, a daughter. But it never occurred to us Ghostrider would produce anything but a son." She pointed at Little Sean. "We were right."

"While all this was going on," she continued. "I took an interest in Jim Walker." Angry Woman snorted and Fawn gave her a stern look. "In the time the two men were there, we got very close. Willow's husband was not happy with the arrangement, but wanted a son, so he agreed to the plan. You must understand that Buffalo Horn was the leader of our clan. His word was law. It was taking a chance, but my father believed it to be the right thing to do. No clan, no bloodline can survive without children."

Angry Woman took over, pointing to Little Sean. "As you can see, the boy looks more white than Indian. Willow's husband could not accept this and killed her in anger, and then put the knife to Buffalo Horn. When that happened, our brothers killed the husband and all his relatives, to take their bad seed from this earth."

Beth, sitting close to Stands Tall, gasped. "All of them?"

Fawn nodded. "There was much anger. To kill only the husband would leave others seeking revenge. By killing all of them, it takes away the threat. A wise person does not kill a bear and then leave the cubs to seek revenge later."

"Seems harsh." Beth was staring out the window. "Maybe this man's relatives didn't like him either and it would have ended with his death."

"You are a child," Angry Woman muttered.

Ignoring Stands Tall's sudden squeezing of her arm in warning, Beth turned her gaze to Angry Woman—a gaze that made the woman take a step back. "I *was* once a child, and I yearn for that again...yearn for that peace. But that child is gone, never to return."

Ellen followed her daughter out the door, placing a hand on her shoulder. "And you're angry too."

"I shouldn't be." She shrugged from under her mother's hand. "I accepted death in the forest, standing over Grandfather's body. I understand anger and revenge."

She tried to hug Beth, but the girl twisted away. But she still stood close. She could tell the women were listening by the door. "What happened then?"

"After finding Buffalo Shield dead, and seeing he'd died by ambush not by battle. I knew much anger. I accepted my death, but not before all the arrows in my pouch tasted blood."

She gave her mother a level gaze. "I did this. If you remember, I am very good with a bow. After I ran out of arrows, I challenged the leader of the renegade Shawnee, knowing I would die...wanting it. Then I was hit from behind and captured."

Ellen's hand went to her mouth, remembering her own captivity that resulted in Beth's birth. "Were you...?"

Beth shook her head. "Later, one of the men dropped a bundle of clothes by me. Hidden inside was a knife so I could escape. The leader's name is Stoneface. He is a cruel and evil man that wants to keep me alive to father his sons, much like the Nez Percé used Sean as a sire... except I was to be a brood mare. His captain is Big Hand, who is jealous of this and wants me dead. Big Hand left the knife so I would escape and then he planned to capture me again and kill me."

"Obviously that didn't happen." Stands Tall came through the door, followed by the two other women. All pretense of not listening was gone. "What happened?"

"At first, I didn't want to run. I'd given up that idea when I avenged Buffalo Shield. There were too many of them and they'd just hunt me down and have their way with me. But then, the anger came. They wanted a chase, so I gave them what they wanted. It was almost dark when I left. Once they followed and could not find me, I went back in the darkness and stole my bow and more arrows. The next morning, I got their attention and led them into the valley of thorns."

Her smile was grim and didn't reach her eyes. "They did not like it there."

"And Night Panther was born." Stands Tall's voice was quiet, barely a whisper while her gaze was on a distant vision.

"If such a creature was ever born?" Beth caught all of them in her gaze, tears running down her cheeks. "If that happened, it was when they killed my grandfather. You talk of revenge, like I am a child? Can you count the warriors you have killed on your two hands? It is not enough for me. I have killed many, wounded more."

She turned her gaze to Angry Woman. "There were thirty arrows in my pouch. All of them tasted blood. I rarely miss. Can you say the same?"

"Something in me thirsts for blood." Her hands crossed over her heart as she continued. "I feel it, want it."

Beth's gaze fell on Stands Tall as she continued. "I am not finished. There is much to be done."

Stands Tall pinned her with a bright gaze. "You should talk to Ghostrider. Though not your blood father, you are joined in spirit and journey the same path. It is not a good place to be."

Beth allowed Ellen to gather her in, hugging her. But there was no compliance, just an unyielding stiffness. She let Beth go while holding her at arm's length and gazing into her eyes. "No. Please, you are too young for this. Let the men handle it. We have soldiers here."

With a sigh, Ellen continued. "I am your mother and will always hold you close to my heart. Listen to these words. You are a young woman. If you must be a warrior, remember to take counsel from others. Weigh it...judge it as you will. Buffalo Shield wasn't the only wise one around you. Remember, even a Night Panther can be trapped and die of foolish choices."

She gently took Beth by the arms. "Come. Let's get you cleaned up and fed. I'd like to enjoy my daughter...if even for a little while."

———

SEAN AND JIM WALKER straddled wooden benches and Shay brought them coffee. Indicating the steaming mugs,

Shay smirked at them. "I'm thinking the bar is closed until we get past this situation." He paused a moment. "And what exactly is the situation?"

Sean laid it out for them. "We had a surveying party attacked. All were killed and the women mutilated. A homestead south of here was treated the same way. Coming back, we discovered the camp of a Cherokee family, all killed except for a baby they'd hidden. All those incidents are getting closer to our homes."

Jim took a sip and grimaced at the black liquid. "How many, do you figure?"

"I thought at least forty, but Beth says half that many."

"What's the story on that?" Jim gave him a doubtful look. "She looked like she'd been through a gauntlet."

"With things getting more dangerous here, we sent her to Saint Louis for schooling. She was accompanied by her adopted grandfather, Buffalo Shield." Sean turned his gaze to his friend. "Buffalo Shield was a Blackfoot medicine man sworn to take my hair and followed me here."

Making a show of looking at Sean's hair, Jim commented. "Since you still have it, that will be a story to be shared later." He gave a pointed look at Shay. "And better shared with a mug of rum."

"I can't believe you sent her to that place. It's nothing but a giant outhouse." Jim Walker continued. "It's obvious they didn't make it.

"I didn't say it was a good decision. My guess would be they turned back. She can be very persuasive."

"Not very...or she wouldn't have got sent." Forcing down another swallow of Shay's coffee, he continued. "Anything else?"

"Not much." Sean shrugged. "The post is well set up for defense. We've made improvements, cleared land in front down to the river. They'd be hard put to get us from any direction. The soldiers are useless in the forest, but behind the fortifications they should be good. Any of the settlers that make it in will be good shots."

Jim nodded. "But we can't stay behind walls forever. If there's only twenty, or so...."

The door to the tavern slammed against the wall as Ellen burst through. "She's gone. Sean, you must find her. She's gone!"

Sean nodded, seemingly unperturbed. "I figured it would happen. Did she take my quiver of arrows?"

Though they'd been estranged and at odds for a while, she still knew him like no other. Ellen studied him a moment and then sat, leaning back against him. Taking his cup, she took a sip. With a panicked look, she started to spit it out and then swallowed with a grimace. "What in hell was that?"

Shay looked offended. "Coffee. I keep it in the pot for Sean. It's only a few weeks old."

She sighed, glancing over her shoulder at Sean. "Actually, she took the arrow pouch and got into the extra roll. Why aren't you concerned? What do you know that I don't?"

"Don't misunderstand. I'm very concerned. Beth knows the forest around here better than all of us. It will be dark in a few hours. I figure she'll do some scouting around." He paused and hugged Ellen to his chest. "You got her cleaned up and fed?"

"I did. And then she disappeared. But she hasn't rested. How can you sit here so uncaring? Our girl is out there in a forest full of renegades."

"I've learned to not worry about things I cannot control. That same forest is home to friendly Cherokee. She'll be fine."

"Those renegades killed Buffalo Shield, and he was a good fighter. If what you said is true about what they do to women...?"

He nodded, though only the men could see it. "I fear you may have lost sight of what your daughter has become. I could see it in her at first glance. She's changed, and is not the little girl that left. Here's what we shall do. Jim, I want you to help the colonel with advice and man the walls if the time comes. Those new Hall rifles you and your ladies have will take a terrible toll on anyone attacking. Hopefully, you won't have to mount a defense. I haven't seen those guns before. How's the range?"

"Not quite as good as the long rifles, since they have that shorter barrel, but good to a hundred yards. As long as we have shot and percussion caps we can do about six shots a minute, which should surprise the hell out of the hostiles. We can cover anything between the walls and the river."

He continued after giving Sean a long look. "Sounds like you won't be here."

"I will not. I'll be leaving before dawn to cut down the odds a bit."

Ellen whirled in his lap to look at him. "And you'll find Beth? She's out there alone—it'll be dark soon."

"I'm thinking she's been in the dark before and can take care of herself." He took a sip of coffee with a sigh. "Besides, I expect she'll find me when the time is right."

Fawn and her sister moved through the door, carrying three children. Fawn came to stand by Walker while Angry Woman found a bench and sat, immediately surrounded by the Cherokee women who helped at the tavern.

"The woman, Stands Tall, is gone and she left the

foundling with us." Fawn gave Walker a pointed look. "I do not want another child right now. Your daughter flattens my breasts every day, there's not much left for another."

Although his mouth opened, Jim wisely didn't comment as she continued. "The other surprise you were going to give Ghostrider is also gone."

"You had more surprises?" He watched his friend a moment. "What else do you have up your sleeve?"

"Well, hell." Walker's voice was exasperated. "The fighting knife you presented to Fawn's father, old Buffalo Horn, found its way back to me. I got it all shined up nice and pretty and was going to present it to you. Then you, being so grateful to me for bringing home your son, would give it back to me as a present. I knew you'd be overwhelmed with the logic of the situation."

Sean nodded, trying to hide his smile. "Sounds reasonable."

"It does?" Walker watched him with a wary eye.

"Yep." Sean gazed out the window at the fading sunlight. "But if what I'm thinking is right, when this is over you'll have a sight more cleaning to do on it."

# Chapter Twenty-Three

BETH LEFT THE POST THROUGH A LITTLE-USED GATE IN the back, nestled between the walls of two cabins. Meant for escape, the only latch was on the inside. Closing the gate, there was no return. Looking at it from the outside, it looked like solid wall.

Once outside, there was barely room to walk between the walls and the bluff behind them. Using this cover she went undetected to the river and turned south. Her plan was to go far enough that she'd be able to cross the river at a shallow ford and come in behind Stoneface and his renegades. What she hadn't planned on was being tired— bone-melting, mind-mushing tired.

Finding a cluster of limestone boulders close to a narrow point in the river, she placed her bow and arrow pouch beside her. Leaning against the smooth rock, her mind whirled with ideas about how to get through the renegades and kill Stoneface. That was her only objective —kill Stoneface. He'd keep himself surrounded by his men, but he might be drawn away. She yawned, fighting the tiredness in her eyes. There was daylight left so she had a little time to waste. She'd need the cover of darkness to carry out her plans.

————

SHE WOKE but didn't move, ashamed of herself for going to sleep. Some warrior she was. Eyes closed, she listened intently for anything out of the ordinary. The river was a muted gurgle as water passed through its rocky path, birds chirped happily as they pressed into the cedars for their nightly perch, while a squirrel scurried in the leaves, barking at some unknown interest. She sighed. The blanket was warm...blanket?

Her eyes snapped open. Stands Tall was sitting beside her, eyes closed, hands folded at her waist.

The older woman's voice was soft. "For a mythical creature, you're not very smart." Stretching her legs, she continued. "Although this is a nice spot to rest."

Taking a quick look around, Beth relaxed. "Why?"

That got her a curious look. "Why what?"

"Take your pick. Why am I not smart? Why did you follow me? Why do you care what I'm doing?" She gave an exasperated sigh. "You know. Why?"

"I followed to slow you down. You are too impulsive, much like Ghostrider. But damn, that man can fight. I'm thinking you can too...that he taught you well. Your advantage is that you look so young and innocent."

Stands Tall leaned forward so she could fully look at the young girl. "But you're no innocent, are you? At least, not anymore."

"It depends on what you call innocent. But no, not anymore."

"Good. We have no time for coddling." Stands Tall continued. "And to answer your question, you left with no blanket to keep you warm, not good planning on your part."

The woman nudged a pouch by her feet. "You didn't bring food to give you strength—unless you planned on drinking the blood of your enemies—which I wouldn't doubt. Never tried it, but I've heard it's nourishing."

"I wasn't planning on needing food. I wasn't aware you needed food in the afterlife." Beth shrugged. "And a blanket? If the White man's Bible is true, it will be plenty warm where I'm going."

Stands Tall laughed at that before continuing. "And you didn't tell anyone of your intentions. You simply left."

What the woman said was true. Thoughts had turned to action and she'd gathered weapons and left. "My intentions are my own. No matter what happens to me, Stoneface must be killed. He is an abomination."

"So your plan is to give your life as long as you can take his in the process? You came out here to die without saying goodbye to your mother, to your adopted father?" She gave her a sly glance. "Or, to your new brother?"

Beth was lost in thought a moment, guilt suddenly weighing her down. The memories of the last few days were the stuff of nightmares, driving her forward with fear and adrenaline. In her anger she'd forgotten family, almost resented her mother trying to help.

She inclined her head to the older woman. "You're right, of course. But I was feeling closed in, losing control. As for the other? Giving my life? It would seem... necessary. I see no other way. Why are you here?"

"A fair question. I made a promise to the Ghostrider. I had a vision that I should watch out for him and try to guide him away from trouble. His anger, much like yours, was leading him in too many directions. He was much confused by the actions of your mother. She'd been talking to a man named Ambrose about taking her to Saint Louis to be with you."

"Ambrose? That rooster?" She almost laughed, shaking her head. "That doesn't make sense. Sean has her heart. I know it."

"I believe that's true. For some reason this Ambrose went to Ghostrider and told him he was taking his woman away and there wasn't anything Ghostrider could do about it, since the woman had agreed to go with him. When Ghostrider objected, Ambrose challenged him."

Beth snorted, visualizing the two men. The lieutenant in all his finery, her adopted father probably slouching at the bar with his friend Shay, mug of coffee in his hand giving the soldier scant attention.

Her voice was sarcastic as she shook her head at the vision in her mind. "How long did it take Sean to kill him?"

"Death comes too easily to your lips." The woman smiled for the first time. "From what I've been told by the women who work in the tavern, about a minute. This Ambrose was a very stupid man, full of his own importance."

"I still don't understand why you are here?" Beth studied the older woman in the fading light.

"I am here to give you an alternative to death. You need to live."

She pondered that a moment before giving the woman a pointed look. "What is your interest in Sean?"

Stands Tall settled back against the stone wall. "Ghostrider is troubled. He has terrible dreams and he is at war with himself. I saw this and tried to help."

"How? Can you talk away his trouble?"

"I slept with him, shared his dreams." At Beth's

flinch, she held up her hand. "Not like that. I gave him a shoulder to rest on...but, only as a friend."

The woman paused a moment. "If you were to ask the Cherokee, I'm called a witch. Many are afraid of me, though I've given them no reason."

A splash in the river jerked their heads toward the sound until a muskrat surfaced in the cold water. They relaxed again.

Beth snorted and threw off the blanket. "We make a pair. A witch and a night panther."

"*Are* you a night panther, someone who turns wild when the sun goes down?" Stands Tall watched with a small smile.

She returned it. "Are you a witch? Do you walk in other people's dreams to guide them?"

Stands Tall looked away. "If you will allow it, I have a suggestion. It's a much better choice than giving your life. You have much to live for."

Beth shrugged. "I accepted my death while standing over the body of my adopted grandfather. When a shadow crossed in front of me, I looked up and saw an eagle floating over us, high in the sky. At first, I thought it was the spirit of my grandfather, but now I think it was waiting for me. It's still waiting. I will not quit. I will not hesitate. Stoneface is a monster and must be killed."

She sighed, closing her eyes and leaning back against the rock. "Although I'm not looking to die needlessly. Dying in the heat and anger of battle is easy. Here? Leaning against this rock, listening to the river pass by, thinking of death? Not so much."

Stands Tall put a hand on her arm. "I'm not asking you to stop what you must do. I'm asking you to be smart. They will attack the post in the morning to try and draw the soldiers out from behind the walls. If their numbers are as you say, they don't have enough to attack directly. Once that fails, and he loses men, I think Stone-face will flee downriver. It is the easiest path. Your best choice is to wait and watch. Let him come to you."

Beth thought about that a moment. "How about if I show myself to him and make him chase me? I don't want to leave it to chance. He may run another direction."

"It's more dangerous." Stands Tall thought a moment, finally nodding. "If he wants you bad enough, that could work."

She thought of the boasts Stoneface had given. "Oh, he wants me." Beth grinned at her, placing a hand over her heart. "He wants to father a race of warriors through me, said he'd wait for me to come of age." She rolled her eyes. "Now, I think he'll just want to kill me. But what of his men? His captain is called Big Hand. What of him?"

"Trust in your adopted father. Let Ghostrider take care of that. He's capable."

Beth watched the older woman a moment, finally broaching the subject. "Do you love Sean? Will you stand in the way of my mother?"

Stands Tall flinched and then settled with a smile. "Don't add me to your list of problems—I don't want the Night Panther on my trail. Ghostrider? I could. Any woman could, he's a good man. But he has eyes only for your mother. If she had not come to her senses and left... then yes, I would be available. There is one thing your mother may never understand that an Indian wife would already know."

She continued in a firm voice. "Ghostrider is a warrior, not a shopkeeper. In that way, you are much like him—maybe because of your Osage father. Your mother needs to understand that and stop trying to change him. She will always have to watch him disappear into the forest and wonder if he'll return. He will often take a path that those who love him cannot follow."

"I'll pass that along." Beth chuckled, pulling the sack of food toward her. "Providing I live."

Stands Tall leaned back against the rock, closing her eyes. "Oh, we'll live, little *Mishipeshu*. I have much to teach you."

# Chapter Twenty-Four

THE NIGHT WAS NOT WITHOUT SOUND. STONEFACE knew his men were scattered through the forest waiting for first light and the attack on the fort. He was anxious to start sending arrows and musket balls toward the Whites and tame Indians cowering behind their walls. In his steady march toward the south, this land was a stumbling block. It was time for an ending to this and begin the journey again toward a new beginning, a new nation, ruled by him.

Meticulously, he began untying the trophies from the handle of the pipe axe. There were too many for his symbolic hatchet of war. One of his men had presented him with a fine lance, with a razor-sharp obsidian point. He stood by a consecrating fire, blackening the handle to match the spear point.

Attaching his trophies to the lance, he gazed toward Jones Mill. There were many women behind those walls. The lance would be filled. Taking a deep breath, he shuddered and walked into the darkness to be alone.

As THE SUN painted the tops of the trees on the ridge behind him, Stoneface raised his lance, heavy with his trophies. Glancing to the right, and then left, he studied his men. Big Hand had found more recruits among the malcontents of the local tribes. Those kinds of men were always available. They wouldn't have the bloodlust of his own warriors, but would do well enough for this.

He slashed the lance downward in a signal to begin and the siege of Jones Mill started. The return fire was impressive, but his men were well entrenched behind boulders and logs just across the river from the fort.

Big Hand came to stand beside him, ignoring musket balls chewing up limbs and biting into tree trunks around him.

"More men came to us. They are eager for the spoils of war. We have enough men to rush the gates if you choose." Big Hand smiled. "We will let the new men lead."

"You have done well." He nodded while watching the fort. "The extra men will be useful. But we still need to lure the soldiers out from behind their walls. Keep up the attack until mid-morning. I can still see people running to the fort for safety. Perhaps we can capture a woman from those to torture in front of the soldiers. That will bring them out."

An arrow, deflected by a low-hanging branch, thumped into a tree beside him burying itself in the bark. He knew it was iron-tipped from the ripping sound it made. Startled, he glanced downriver, following the smoke from the muskets that hung in the air along the banks. A tall, young girl stood on the other side of the river, holding a bow.

He pointed her out to his lieutenant. "See? We are favored by the spirits. The young Night Panther, daughter to the Ghostrider, has returned for us. Keep firing on the fort, but not so much we run out of powder and shot. Try to keep them pinned inside their walls. I will capture this demon and bring her back."

Big Hand stopped Stoneface. "Let me do this. She gave me much dishonor when she got away. It won't happen again."

An arrow grazed his arm, leaving a thin line of blood before disappearing into the brush behind him. Absently rubbing the shallow wound, Big Hand continued. "Prepare the torture post. Have the men bring a woman to put on the post. That will bring the Ghostrider out from the walls so we can kill him. If you wait until I return with her, she can watch. As you said before, that will break her, and you can do as you wish. Once Ghostrider is dead, the fort will be ours for the taking."

When Stoneface nodded, Big Hand gave a high, keening cry and burst across the shallows of the river in long strides, rejoicing in the startled look the girl gave him before she turned and ran. She chose an easy path, probably thinking it would help her speed. But he knew she would be no match for his strength. Soon she would be his.

———

BETH TRIED to send an arrow into Stoneface's guts, but it was a long shot—she tried again. She missed! Twice. As she turned to run, she chided herself. She would use Stands Tall's plan after all. She ran down the beaten path alongside the stream. Glancing over her shoulder, she saw it was Big Hand, not Stoneface, and he was gaining. He was faster than she anticipated. Fear made her start breathing in time with her footfalls. Realizing her mistake, she willed herself to take deep breaths. This was no time to get winded. Looking back, she saw he'd gained a little more ground.

Any time you look back while running, you lose a step. She knew this from running the trails against the Cherokee boys and girls. The more philosophical rule is if you're looking back, you can't look forward. Recent rains had eroded the trail. When her foot hit a crack in the earth, she sprawled awkwardly on her face, dropping her bow as she tried to catch herself.

Leaping to her feet, he was almost upon her. Abandoning her bow, she ran again. Only this time the fear was real, and the white-hot pain in her ankle slowed her down. He was close and there wasn't anything she could do about it. The sound of their footfalls pounded in her ears.

Ahead were two boulders and a clearing beyond. She gripped her knife, ready to make a stand. Slowing down as she passed the rocks, she heard his shout of triumph as he saw her within his reach.

The shout turned into a surprised curse as he tripped on the rawhide rope hidden in the dirt and suddenly stretched taut by Stands Tall. As he sprawled in the dirt, she leaped forward and stunned him with a blow to the head.

"Well," Stands Tall spoke as she gathered up her rope. "That was easier than I thought it would be."

"It's the wrong man. This is his lieutenant, Big Hand."

"Why this one?"

"He wants me too. It was him and a few of his men that I led through the valley of thorns. He had to return to Stoneface a beaten cur. I don't think he likes me much." Beth was still trying to catch her breath, holding her side and panting. As the man groaned and stirred, she asked. "What now?"

"I'm sure he helped rape and kill those women." Stands Tall paused a moment and then continued. "Help me drag him over by the river. The earth is soft there."

Dragging the heavy man by his heels proved harder than they thought. Finally, he was spread-eagled on the bank. They'd fashioned stakes to be driven into the ground with flat rocks. Once that was done, his wrists and ankles were tied securely with pieces cut from the rawhide rope.

Beth watched curiously for a moment, hand on the knife at her waist. "Why this? Why don't we kill him now?"

"Not yet my little bloodthirsty friend. He will serve a purpose before he dies. What happens next will be for the innocents he has killed. Women from the tribes will be coming to this spot soon, brought by my signal fire. Each will inflict a cut just big enough to attract insects."

Stands Tall walked to her duffel and pulled out a long knife.

Beth watched curiously. "Isn't that Sean's fighting knife?"

"No. One like it. I borrowed it from his friend. It is very sharp." She looked at Beth and nodded toward the trail. "Go now. This dog will awaken soon, and I must be ready."

Beth watched as the woman began gathering sticks to start a fire. "Are you going to burn him?"

"No. Just a part of him. The rest will be up to the ants and scavengers when we are through with him. It will be a fitting end for what he has done."

They were interrupted by the increased sound of

gunfire echoing through the hills. Both whirled toward the sound.

Stands Tall spoke with a grim expression. "They are attacking hard. Now go. Ghostrider needs your help, but be careful. If you're captured again, it won't end well."

"I won't be captured." Checking to make sure her arrow pouch was secure and reminding herself to pick up her bow on the way back, she moved to Stands Tall and embraced her. "Be careful Big Hand doesn't break his bonds. He is very strong."

Stands Tall glanced at the man struggling on the ground. "I'm counting on him being strong. I don't want him to die too soon."

———

SEAN STOOD with Jim Walker near the front gate. They'd met after walking among the defenders and telling them to stop shooting. There was no point in wasting powder and shot at men hiding in the forest beyond the river. It was better to let those attacking them run low on munitions first.

Colonel Thompson strode up to them. "What's going on? Why stop fighting?"

"There is no point in wasting bullets. That's what they want." He paused a moment, looking around at the defenders. "Look. We're probably going to be at this awhile. You might ask the women to organize food and coffee—no rum. We'll eat in shifts so the walls are always defended. Until something changes, we're kinda at an impasse. They can't get at us in the fort, and we can't go out and get them without suffering too many casualties."

"I don't agree." The colonel shook his head. "I should

form the troop and march against them. We can wipe them out with superior numbers."

Sean smiled at him. "That's a tactic the Redcoats used against the colonials. How'd that work out for them?"

When the man started to argue, Walker interrupted, holding up his hand between the two men. "Think about it, Colonel. They own the forest, with good cover, and you'd have to cross that river to get at them. I know it's shallow, but it has a slick bottom. The men would have to go slow to keep from falling and getting their powder wet. For the ones out there in the trees, it'd be like shooting ducks on a pond. Your advantage is these walls. Their advantage is the river. Let them make the first mistake, Colonel. We got nothing but time."

The soldier shook his head slowly. "This isn't my kind of war. I don't have the patience for it. I'm thinking these renegades are the ones who killed my family and I want to go after them. It's hard to know what to do."

"Not your fault, Colonel. You were just taught wrong." Sean grinned at him. "Now if you fail to adapt, that is your fault. I have no control over you or your men. It's up to you."

"What about Beth?" Sean flinched. Quiet as always, Ellen had come up behind him.

She put her arm around his waist as he spoke to her. "I'm sure she can take care of herself." He watched Walker move away to be joined by his women. "That girl is more at home out there than within these walls."

Walker was by the gate, looking through a port and motioning toward them. "Let go see what's going on."

# Chapter Twenty-Five

THE SHOOTING FROM THE FOREST HAD STOPPED AS Sean and Jim Walker stood in the portal of the main gate. As they watched, a group of braves brought a struggling Cherokee man and woman across the shallows, slipping on the wet rocks and some falling in the water.

"Well, hell." Sean shook his head, glancing at his friend.

They were interrupted by one of the warriors striding a few feet forward from the group before shouting at them. "We want the Ghostrider. If the coward does not come out, this woman will die."

Sean called to him. "Are you the one called Stoneface?"

The man shook his lance hard. "I am Stoneface, follower of the great Black Hoof of the Shawnee—who is brother to Tecumseh."

He grinned at Jim Walker. They both knew how the game was played. To anger an opponent is to have an advantage over them. Anyone who'd been to the far lands of the upper Missouri or Rendezvous with trappers and Indians, knew hurling insults were just part of the dance.

"I have heard of the prophet Black Hoof who makes loud noises and frightens children. I also know of Stoneface, who is a killer of small children and sleeps with dogs because he cannot satisfy a woman. I will attend to you in a moment."

That brought on a cacophony of hooting and whistles from the fort. Before they could react, Angry Woman brushed past them through the door to lift her dress at the warriors and then spit at them. No greater insult could have been done.

"Oh," Jim said. "That was a good one."

Shaking his head, Sean stepped inside the gate and spoke to the colonel. "I'm going out there to take care of Stoneface. His men are well within range now. When I take off my hat, I want one volley. Clear out everyone surrounding me and Stoneface."

He turned to Dave. "Can your wives help with their new rifles? They need to take out the men holding the man and woman. It should be pretty easy."

"You're going down there? Alone?"

He turned to his friend. "I am. I need you to take care of the defense and no matter what happens to me, keep the hostiles out at all costs. And keep Ellen from doing anything stupid."

"Why?" Jim replied. "Do you want to be the only one being stupid? It's a risky thing you're doing."

Handing his bow to Jim, he said. "I have very few friends. You are one. Another is down there with his wife, waiting for rescue. I have to go."

Jim shook his head and then nodded. "All right. We'll cover you. If you fight one-on-one, we won't interfere. Anything else and we'll cut them down. Good luck to you. And don't forget you have a son to come back to."

Glancing around the compound, he noticed Ellen walking toward the walls with her new friends, carrying her rifle. He shook hands with Jim and began the walk down toward the river. He was confident he could defeat Stoneface, but would be a fool to think it would be easy. And there was always the unknown happenstance— turning an ankle, tripping, any of a hundred things that could go wrong. And the worst of all. No matter how good you are, there is always someone better. Always.

He hadn't gone far when he heard the soft padding of footfalls behind him. Ellen appeared at his side, trying to match his strides. He slowed a little so she wouldn't appear awkward. "You sure about this?"

"It's where I belong. I can watch your back."

"Things may go wrong."

"Then we'll go down together." Her eyes were wet when she glanced at him. "Now, don't waste time thinking of me. Think of that bastard you're going to kill. If he lives, he'll find Beth."

They stopped within a few feet of the preening and strutting Shawnee, who was pacing in front of his men. Glancing at Red Eagle, standing defiant and still struggling with his captors, he made a slight spreading motion with his hands. The man immediately muttered to his wife, and they moved just enough to give some separation between them and their captors.

Stoneface drove his spear into the ground so hard, one of his trophies came loose and landed in front of them. At one glance and recognizing what it was, Ellen hissed in anger and kicked it back toward Stoneface.

The Indian pulled his knife from a scabbard tied around his hips. "I am surprised you came, Ghostrider.

Your death will be a remembered thing. I will send your hair north to the Blackfoot so they can celebrate."

Sean nodded. "I came because I made a promise to a small boy—a boy that gutted one of your mighty warriors before your brave men killed him and his family. Be sure to sing your song of bravery to the Great Spirit when you see him. I'm sure he'll be impressed."

The Shawnee pointed his knife at Sean. "Pull your knife, Ghostrider. This day I will have this Cherokee woman." He paused and looked at Ellen. "And your White woman."

Ellen snorted and spit at the man's feet.

"Kneel." Sean spoke softly to her and was surprised when Ellen kneeled immediately. Sighing, he made a show of taking off his hat to ready himself for battle.

Moments later a volley came from the walls of the fort and men dropped all around them. Freed from their captors, Red Eagle hustled his wife toward the walls. Sean motioned him away when he tried to stop. When one man stepped out to stop them, Ellen shot him in the face from her position on the ground. One more warrior lifted his tomahawk to throw at her and was immediately dropped with another shot from the walls. It was a message well sent. The rest of Stoneface's men stood nervously, unsure whether to fight or run.

With a metallic ringing sound, Sean pulled his fighting knife from its metal scabbard. "Now, I will attend to you."

The ground was soft and level with few obstructions for them to trip over. At one glance, Sean knew he couldn't match this man with strength—the Shawnee was built like a bull.

When Stoneface charged forward, it was all power meant to bowl over his opponent and force him to the ground. Sean didn't oblige, sliding out of the way at the last moment and leaving a deep cut on the Shawnee's thigh.

Stoneface stopped and looked at his leg. "You think to stop me with little cuts? Is this how you killed the Blackfoot, by running away?"

"You are a killer of helpless women and children," Sean answered. "How many men have you killed, Stoneface? Any at all, or do your men do that for you?"

With a roar, the man rushed him again, while Sean stepped away again leaving another cut as he passed by. After a few minutes of the warrior trying to rush after him, Sean could see he was tiring. Most fights of any kind take very little time. Someone is always stronger or has some advantage. This one had taken longer than most, simply because he wanted to inflict pain on the man. And the Shawnee was tiring from losing blood.

Stoneface turned and looked at his men. "Take him."

Just as the warriors were surging forward, they were stopped by a high, keening cry.

One of the men yelled, "Mishipeshu!" At this, the man turned and fled across the river. The rest backed away.

As Stoneface turned toward the sound, he was hit in the chest with an arrow that nearly passed through him. Astonished, he watched the girl stalking toward him. He was hit with two more arrows before he fell, eyes wide open staring at the girl.

Beth stalked up and stood over the man. "You killed my grandfather Buffalo Shield. Remember his name in the afterlife. His spirit will now rest easy in the spirit land."

It was Sean's turn to be astonished. He'd never seen

such anger in anyone as what he was seeing in his adopted daughter.

She walked past the dying Stoneface toward the other warriors. They took another step back when she pointed at them with her bow. "I am Mishipeshu, Night Panther of the Cherokee and the Osage." She pointed at the body of Stoneface. "Take this dog with you and leave this land. Do not return."

In a silent shuffle, the men complied.

When they'd crossed the river and disappeared into the forest, Beth turned to her shocked mother and adopted father. "I'm sorry you saw that. I was mad and saw no reason to let the fight go on, although I'm sure Ghostrider would have won."

Sean nodded. "That was some fine shooting. And the warriors? I take it they've seen you before?"

"Some of them have—I'm sure the story spread."

"I..." Ellen gave her head a slight shake, still trying to find her voice. "Are you possessed?"

Beth gave an impish smile. "No, but don't tell anyone."

Jim Walker came strolling up with Fawn and Angry Woman. "Who taught you to shoot a bow like that?"

She pointed at Sean. "He did, and Buffalo Shield."

Jim grinned at her. "Where'd you get that temper?"

Beth pointed at her mother and smiled. "That's all hers, but it's useful at times."

As they turned back toward the gates, Jim looked around at the deserted ground around them and nodded. "I reckon so."

# Chapter Twenty-Six

IT WAS CROWDED IN SHAY'S TAVERN WHEN SEAN PAUSED at the doorstep. Turning to look behind him, he could see the gate was open and a normal number of people coming and going through it, back to doing their normal business as usual. A couple of sentries kept watch along the walls, and he knew people from the outlying cabins had returned to their homes. It was moving toward evening and he was tired—and satisfied with how the day had gone, and anxious to open a new chapter in his life.

Stands Tall trudged wearily through the gates, so he waited until she arrived. "You took care of the burial?"

"Let's wait until we are inside. The others should know."

He shrugged and let her precede him inside. Shay had shooed out the barflies and occasional drinkers, knowing there was still much to discuss. It had been an eventful day.

Leaning with his elbows on the bar and facing his friends, he called for their attention. "We have some things to decide, or at least start the discussion, but first I think Stands Tall needs to tell us her news."

"It is done." She started in a tired voice, but gained strength as she continued. "The trophies from Stone-face's lance have been buried with a ceremony by the women of the Cherokee."

Her sigh spoke volumes about what they'd found. "There were maybe fifteen different..." She paused a moment. "...trophies. We hope their spirits may rest now."

Beth spoke up softly. "Big Hand?"

Stands Tall shrugged. "Still alive, though I doubt he lasts through the night. The women are keeping watch." She glanced at Beth. "It was a punishment I'd hoped to give Stoneface."

When Sean and Jim had heard of the fate of Big Hand, they'd both cringed a little although it was well known that if it came down to it...it was much better to be killed in battle than to be captured by the women of any tribe. They were much more brutal and creative.

Sean took a gulp of flip. "All right. I guess we'll leave that to the women, assuming he's too weak to break free and harm anyone?"

At a nod from Stands Tall, he continued. "The next thing we need to talk about is when we leave. There is a good place north of here where the prairie meets the foothills. I found a couple of good springs we could build a trading post close to. There is game and fish. I think in a year or so, we could establish a trade between Kawsmouth to the north, and posts along the Arkansas border."

"What needs to be done?" Jim Walker spoke up from where he sat between two women. "Is it close to that Nesbitt fella we met? He might object."

"I met Miller Nesbitt and wasn't impressed. He and his men can stay around or leave."

"Well to be right accurate," Walker said. "He's got less men than he started with, thanks to Angry Woman."

"It's a shame to lose good people," Shay spoke up. "Can't you be persuaded to stay?"

Ellen spoke up. "Don't the women have a say in this?" She glanced around the room. Fawn and Angry Woman shrugged noncommittally, and Beth just smiled at her. Ellen shook her head. "Thanks for the help, ladies."

Sean grinned at them, nodding his acceptance. "We'll try to head out day after tomorrow. That will give us time for packing and farewells."

It was near dark when they strolled out of the tavern. Jim Walker led his entourage toward an empty cabin, while Beth walked away in deep discussion with Stands Tall.

"Can I get my husband to spend a night under my roof?" Ellen was already pulling him toward the cabin.

"Husband?" He held her close. "If that's a proposal, then yes. And wild horses couldn't keep me away."

———

AT FALSE DAWN, two days later, the little group was gathered at the gate preparing to leave. Sean looked them over and could see they were waiting on him to lead out. In a way, he hated to go. The surrounding forest was his home, he was used to it and he knew Ellen was. But his heart told him they needed a new beginning and he was ready, excited to take the trail. His wandering days were over and his friend Jim Walker had expressed the same sentiment. Of course, both having small children had a lot to do with it.

Ellen moved her horse next to his, holding Little Sean in a carrier Fawn had made for her. She glanced at the horse Sean was riding. "Where is Thunder?"

Sean gave her a humorous look. "Well, it seems our resident Night Panther decided she needed a warhorse—something more in keeping with her new status in life." He shrugged. "In truth, Thunder is getting a little slow and the years are starting to work on him. They'll be fine together."

"Still...I worry."

"Mothers always worry. She'll be along, soon enough."

With one more glance behind, he booted his horse in the flanks and started the little cavalcade north toward their new beginning.

———

THE SUN PEEKED through the trees on the mountain to the east when Beth stepped out on a rock ledge for her morning prayer. Hills and mist-shrouded valleys stretched out below her. She kneeled in her buckskin dress waiting as the first light winked over the crest of the mountain. Gazing around her, the peace of the forest flowed through her. The fragrance of honeysuckle and jasmine carried on the breeze along with the sleepy chirps of birds waking for the new day.

She no longer resisted the blood that coursed through her veins. Instead, she embraced the knowledge. She raised her face to the new day and began her traditional Osage morning prayer of supplication and thanks. Once through with those, she gave another prayer.

"Oh great Wakonta, Spirit of the Fathers. My blood holds two wolves, each fighting for dominance. On one side I am Niukonska, an Osage Child of the Middle

Waters. I have no clan, my blood is not pure, and yet I feel for my brothers and sisters of the forest."

"On the other I am Beth, daughter of Ellen, adopted daughter of my father, Ghostrider. My adopted grandfather, the great Blackfoot warrior Buffalo Shield, has joined his family in the spirit land, no longer walking this earth. The Ghostrider has taken back his woman and embraced a new son. They are content. The medicine woman Stands Tall has shared her power and that mystery runs through my blood. This land is at peace. But it shall not last."

"When the blood of the two wolves comes together in my heart, I become *Mishipeshu*. There is much anger with this and I frighten myself. Soon the Night Panther must again walk among her people and I don't know what that will bring."

Her hands stretched to the sky as the morning sunbathed her face. "My loved ones are settled. They all have mates. Who will come for me?" She felt a tear course its way down her cheek and with an angry flick of her head sent it away. "Who will come to stand by me?"

She finally gave a strong sigh. "I am a child to the Whites—a woman to my Indian brothers. Much have I seen and endured, but it made me strong. I am *Mishipeshu*, feared among the People. Of the two wolves on my shoulders, I feed both and survive.

"I am Beth Mackey, daughter to Ellen and adopted daughter to the Ghostrider—adopted granddaughter to Buffalo Shield and blood sister to Stands Tall. All these things are true. And as all my elders and teachers advise me, I will wait."

Standing, she brushed off her dress. With a small smile, she whispered. "But not long. Not long."

# Notes from the Author

Some poetic license is taken in turning the Mishipeshu into a night panther.

The mythical Mishipeshu, whose direct translation is Great Lynx, was a mythical creature affiliated with the Ojibwe, Algonquin, Ottawa, Menominee, Creek Tribes, and the Shawnee. Also known as a water panther or underwater panther.

Mythical creatures, then and now, are a great way of explaining things we don't understand.

The antagonist Stoneface is a fictional character patterned after the fundamentalist Shawnee Black Hoof, a brother to the moderate Tecumseh. After the seven-year Creek war he and his followers moved south toward a land called Oklahoma.

Around 1820, an estimated 4000 Cherokee lived in Southwest Missouri and Northwest Arkansas. Thousands of black bear were killed by Indian and White trappers for bear oil. This was traded, sold and shipped to New Orleans.

Enemies of the Cherokee were the Osage and

Delaware. The Delaware were congregated around Springfield, Missouri, at Anderson's Post.

The Osage empire covered a portion Arkansas, Missouri, Oklahoma, and Kansas. Although a major part of the Ozark Plateau was given up in a treaty with the federal government in 1808, they still claimed the right to hunt all this territory.

Darrel Sparkman

# A Look at: Quinlan's Law
## By Darrel Sparkman

**The endless summer of 1879 baked the soul out of Kansas—and out of every man riding it.**

Across the wind-scoured plains of eastern Kansas, the sun bleached the color from everything it touched. Quinlan Barrett figured he'd seen his share of killing. After a scrape with rustlers, he was ready to hang up his guns and start fresh. Falling under the spell of Consuela Pinder wasn't part of the plan.

Then Consuela was taken—stolen by Macrae, a madman with a taste for cruelty and a gang trafficking women across the border into old Mexico.

Quin has worn a badge in every corner of the frontier: Deputy U.S. Marshal in Indian Territory, railroad detective on the KATY, livestock inspector in the Kansas City stockyards. These days, that badge rides deep in his pocket. But when the trail runs red, it's not duty that calls him back—it's a promise he intends to keep.

With the scout Kiowa Smith, the Exoduster Zeke Fontenot, and a few hardened veterans of the Cherokee Brigade, Quinlan Barrett saddles up once more. Because there's killing to be done —and a woman to bring home.

*Some promises can only be kept in blood.*

***AVAILABLE DECEMBER 2025***

# About the Author

Darrel Sparkman is an award-winning author of novels, novellas, and short stories. He's been included in three western anthologies, worked as a feature writer for *Saddlebag Dispatches* and blogged a short time for *Sundown Press*.

His ideas come from a diverse past of serving as a combat search and rescue helicopter crewman in Vietnam and volunteer Emergency Medical Technician First Responder. He has worked as a professional photographer, computer repair tech, and was once part-owner of a commercial greenhouse operation and flower shop.

Darrel is enjoying semi-retirement and finally has that job that wakes him up every day—with a smile on his face.

www.darrelsparkmanbooks.com